Jessica appreciated that he could make her laugh, especially after her mini meltdown.

She suspected the man could handle himself in any situation. "Good luck. Figure out your mystery. Then bring me my caramelly coffee, and we'll talk more."

He paused with one hand on the fence's top railing. "You're sure you're okay?"

"I will be."

Jessica watched him stride away.

She could see why the Gardner ladies had the hots for him.

And why she had to keep her guard up around his take-charge strength and surprisingly gentle compassion. She couldn't do a relationship again. Not even with a good man like Garrett. She'd had love. She'd been growing her family. She'd planned a future. And every last bit of it had been violently taken from her.

She was a survivor.

She could live her life. Be useful. Find joy and a purpose with her dogs.

But she wasn't strong enough to love and lose again.

T0008815

SHADOW SURVIVORS

USA TODAY Bestselling Author

JULIE MILLER

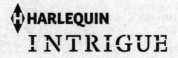

HARLEQUIN

INTRIGUE

If you purchased this book without a cover you should be aware that this book is stolen property. It was reported as "unsold and destroyed" to the publisher, and neither the author nor the publisher has received any payment for this "stripped book."

For Daisy and Teddy—our two doodlebugs. Both blind in one eye. A black Poodle mix, a white Poodle mix. An introvert and an extrovert. One who will never sit in your lap to be petted but who will never turn her nose up at a treat. And the other who can't get enough personal attention and who will take a tummy rub over a treat any day. One who enjoys her solitude, and one who panics when he's left alone. One who was returned to the shelter twice before finding his forever home with us, and the other who was never wanted at all until she was rescued from a horrible situation. You two are so good for each other, and you're good for us. You have to be a special dog to be a Miller dog. Mama loves you both.

HARLEQUIN®
INTRIGUE™

Recycling programs for this product may not exist in your area.

ISBN-13: 978-1-335-59160-9

Shadow Survivors

Copyright © 2024 by Julie Miller

For questions and comments about the quality of this book, please contact us at CustomerService@Harlequin.com.

TM and ® are trademarks of Harlequin Enterprises ULC.

Harlequin Enterprises ULC
22 Adelaide St. West, 41st Floor
Toronto, Ontario M5H 4E3, Canada
www.Harlequin.com

Printed in Lithuania

MIX
Paper | Supporting responsible forestry
FSC® C021394

Julie Miller is an award-winning *USA TODAY* bestselling author of breathtaking romantic suspense—with a National Readers' Choice Award and a Daphne du Maurier Award, among other prizes. She has also earned an *RT Book Reviews Career Achievement Award*. For a complete list of her books, monthly newsletter and more, go to juliemiller.org.

Visit the Author Profile page at Harlequin.com.

CAST OF CHARACTERS

Jessica "Jessie" Bennington—She survived tragedy and has built herself a new life rescuing and training dogs at K-9 Ranch. Her faithful service dog, Shadow, is her constant companion and helps with her panic attacks. Her dogs give her a purpose; the local silver fox deputy gives her friendship. Can she move past her fears to embrace an unexpected family? And protect them from the evil hunting them down?

Deputy Garrett Caldwell—The widower and retired army sniper has poured himself into his career with the Jackson County Sheriff's Department. Now entering his fifties, he's realizing all the things missing from his life—a family, a strong woman by his side, love. He'll content himself with his friendship with Jessie if that's the only way he can be with her. But he wants so much more—and he'll put his life on the line to protect their future.

Shadow—This German shepherd mix is the grand old man of the ranch. The smartest and most versatile of all Jessie's dogs.

Nate and Abby—An Amber Alert has been issued for the children.

Kai Olivera—The skull tattooed on his bald head isn't the scariest thing about him.

Conor Wildman—KCPD detective.

Chapter One

Shadow growled.

Tensing, Jessica Bennington looked over at her German shepherd mix with the graying muzzle, who had just risen from his sunny spot in the grass and gone on alert.

Now what? The dogs at her K-9 Ranch rescue and training center had raised a ruckus late last night, too. They had all been locked up in their kennels, the barn, or the house, so she hadn't been worried about one of them getting into trouble. She'd thrown a jacket on over her pajamas and slipped into a pair of sneakers, grabbed a flashlight and Shadow, and gone out to investigate. But by the time she'd checked each and every one of them, the hubbub had died down. One must have seen a fox or a raccoon and barked, then the others would have joined in because no self-respecting dog wanted to be left out of sounding the alarm. Other than a few extroverts who seized the opportunity to get some petting, they'd immediately settled for the night. But since her own K-9 partner hadn't alerted to anything unusual, Jessica had dismissed any threat, walked back to the house, and had fallen into bed.

But Shadow was alerting this morning. His ears flicked toward the sound that only a dog could hear, his dark eyes riveted to movement in the distance that only a dog could see.

She hated that growl. It was the sound of danger. A threat. Sometimes, even death. It was the sound of salvation and sacrifice.

It was the sound of the nightmare she'd lived with for twelve long years.

She instinctively splayed her fingers over her belly and the scars beneath her jeans. There was nothing to protect there anymore. There never would be.

Barely aware of the younger dog she'd been working with taking his cue from Shadow and turning toward the perceived threat, Jessica felt her blood pressure spike. Both dogs faced the pines and pin oaks that formed a windbreak and offered some much-needed privacy around the small acreage outside of Kansas City, Missouri. She couldn't afford to be paralyzed by the memories that assailed her. She had to push them aside. She had to let Shadow do what she'd trained him to do. She could overcome. She could survive this moment, just like she had so many others.

Jessica forced out a calming breath and stepped up beside the rescue dog that had been her protector, emotional support, and most loyal companion these past ten years. "What is it, boy?"

She sensed the tension vibrating through Shadow but knew he wouldn't charge off to investigate unless she gave him the command to do so. Shadow's black-and-tan coat was longer than a pure-blooded shepherd, thanks to the indefinite parentage of running with a pack until he'd been taken to a shelter in Kansas City and Jessica had picked him to be her first rescue. But that shaggy coat had been a comfort on more than one occasion in the ten years she'd had him. It would be now, too. She slid her fingers from her stomach into the thick fur atop his head, absorbing his heat, finding strength in knowing he was as devoted to her as she was to him.

She would never again be alone and helpless and unable to save the ones she loved.

Not with Shadow by her side.

Jessica finally heard the deep bark of one of her patrol dogs in the distance and relaxed a fraction. Her dogs were doing their jobs. That loud woof was Rex, a big, furry galoot of laziness and curiosity. He was more noise than fight—just the way she'd trained the gentle giant to behave. He wasn't much of a people dog, but he did enjoy roaming the six acres of her Shadow Protectors Ranch. A natural herder and caretaker, the Anatolian had adopted her three goats, a barn cat, and an abandoned litter of possums over the years. Had he found some other critter he wanted to take home to his stall in the barn? While Rex had yet to choose a person he liked well enough to bond with, he made a great deterrent to trespassers who wandered onto her land.

That's when she heard Toby's excited bark joining the chorus. Toby was the opposite of Rex in terms of personality. The black Lab wanted to be friends with everyone, hence he was no kind of guard dog at all. But he was a great noisemaker and loved to be in on the action. Toby and Rex had definitely discovered something near her property line to the west.

Mollie Crane, the client she'd been working with, sidled up beside Jessica, tucking her short dark-brown hair behind her ears. "Is something wrong?"

The younger woman she was helping was one breath away from a panic attack. The man she'd said she needed protection from had really done a number on her. Her fingers brushed against Jessica's elbow instead of reaching for Magnus, the dark faced Belgian Malinois who was training to be her service dog. "Is someone out there? Is it that grumpy old man who works for you? Or his grandson who cleans out the kennels? I'm not sure I like him. He's *too* friendly. Can someone be too friendly? I like his grandfather better. He's not very chatty, but at least he doesn't force me into a conversation or try to flirt with me."

Jessica squeezed her hand over Mollie's fingers to calm her. "Easy, Mollie. Take a breath." She breathed deeply, once, twice, with the woman, who was twenty years her junior. It was easier to control her own fears when she had her dogs or someone else to worry about. "Shadow's on alert because he hears and smells something atypical in his world. The dogs all know Mr. Hauck and his grandson, Soren. This is something different."

"An intruder? Could someone have followed me out here from the city? Wouldn't we have heard them pulling up the driveway?" She was one thought away from hyperventilating. Mollie's fingers were still clenched around Jessica's elbow as she looked down at her dog.

"Why isn't Magnus barking? Is it because he's deaf in one ear? Does he not hear the threat? He's not going to be able to protect me, is he?"

Jessica glanced down at the Belgian Malinois who'd washed out of the Army's K-9 Corps because of chronic ear infections and hearing loss. "He's aware. Believe me, he sees more with those eyes than you or I ever will. But he's still in training. We'll get him where you need him to be. Don't worry. For now, let him be a comfort to you—something to focus on besides your fear." She tried to pull away. "I really need to go. If they've trapped a skunk, or there is someone—"

"Okay, um, Magnus?" Mollie picked up the Malinois's leash off the dry grass that hadn't had enough spring rain yet to turn green.

"Not like that." Jessica spared a moment to help her client. "You're the boss. He wants to please you. If you're *not* the boss, he's going to please himself." Jessica demonstrated. "Shadow, sit." She raised her hand. "Down." The shepherd's black nose stayed in the air, even as he eased his creaky joints to the ground. "Stay," she added, although he'd already obeyed her visual cues. She nodded to Mollie. "Now, you tell Magnus."

Mollie dutifully raised her hand. "Magnus. Sit." The young, muscular dog tipped his nose up to her and plopped his haunches on the ground. "He did it!" Mollie's success transformed her wary expression into a shy smile. "Good boy." She scratched the dog around his limp ear. "Now what?"

Although Jessica had spent a fortune to fence in the entire acreage to keep her dogs off the gravel roads and nearby state highway, she knew that a human being could either climb the fence or cut through it if they were agile enough and determined to trespass. "Mollie, I need to go." She needed to check out the hullabaloo as much as Shadow wanted to. "Take Magnus back to the barn and do some bonding with him. You've both had a good training session this morning and need a break."

Mollie's hands fisted around the leash. "By myself?"

"Sweetie, he chose you that first day you came to the ranch. Remember? He came right up to you and sat on your foot? He wants you to give him a chance to be the dog you need." Jessica shrugged, anxious to get to her dogs to make sure they were safe, but equally worried about jeopardizing Mollie's training. Although she earned good money training dogs for several paying clients, she had an affinity for women like Mollie, who *needed* a companion to help her feel safe. Mollie lived on a small budget, working as a waitress at a diner in Kansas City. But because of Jessica's own background with violence, she charged Mollie only a fraction of her regular fee. She would have given the young woman the dog and trained them for free, but she'd discovered she was as much a therapist as a trainer. Jessica understood that Mollie needed to make her own way in the world. She needed to build the confidence that had been stripped away from her by her past, and Jessica would do whatever was necessary to help. "Play a game with Magnus," she advised. "Get on the ground with him and pet him. There are treats and toys in the last cabinet out in the barn." She reached into the pocket of her jeans and pulled out her ring of work keys. She held up a small padlock key. "Here. This will unlock the cabinet."

"Okay. I can do this, right?" Mollie fisted her hand around the keys.

Jessica softened her tone and squeezed the other woman's fist. "Yes, you can. Love Magnus. Earn his trust. Provide his food, leadership, entertainment and comfort, and he will be your best friend—the most loyal friend you will ever have. Answering the specific commands you need will come later." She gave the other woman's shoulder one more squeeze before pulling away. "Please. I need to see what's going on. I need to make sure none of my protectors are getting themselves into trouble."

Mollie nodded, accepting the mission Jessica had given her. Using a hand signal to get the tan dog's attention focused on her, she spoke in a surprisingly firm voice. "Magnus, heel." Then she tugged on the leash and the dog fell into step beside her.

"Just like that. Good job. You'll be safe in the barn."

Shadow remained at her feet, but his nose and ears indicated he was anxious to check out the disturbance, too. Could the ex-husband Mollie was so afraid of have found her here, eight miles outside the KC city limits? Jessica released her dog from his stay command. "Shadow, seek."

Needing no more encouragement, he took off at a loping run, and Jessica jogged to keep pace with him. She slowed as they reached the trees. Although the oaks were just beginning to bud and posed no obstacle, the evergreens had full, heavy branches she had to push her way through. She worried when Shadow dashed beyond her sight. "Shadow?" The barking tripled as the dog joined Rex and Toby.

Jessica pushed aside the last branch, stopped in her tracks and cursed on a deep sigh. "This isn't good."

Chapter Two

A protective anger pushed aside Jessica's fear and she hurried her stride to approach the trio of dogs barking at the white-haired neighbor swinging the barrel of her shotgun from one dog to the next from her side of the fence. "Miss Eloise? Good morning."

"Don't *good morning* me. Your mutts are a terror, Jessica Bennington! An absolute terror." Eloise Gardner had once been a tall woman. But now she was stooped with age and frail enough that she panted from the exertion of holding up the heavy gun and walking the quarter mile from her house to the fence. She nodded toward the broken railing that butted up against Jessica's chain-link fence. "Look what they did to my fence."

The log fence was little more than faded wood and chipped white paint after years of weather and neglect. The top rail looked as though it had rotted through and splintered in half beneath the weight of someone leaning against it or stepping onto it. Or maybe it had finally surrendered under its own weight to age and decay.

Keeping her demeanor calm so the dogs would obey her, Jessica called them to her side. "Rex! Toby! Shadow!

Come." The three dogs lined up beside her, and with a set of nonverbal commands, they sat and lay down. Jessica kept her arm out at a 45-degree angle from her body to make them stay put. Trying not to panic that the shotgun was pointed in her direction now, as well, Jessica drummed up a smile and a civil tone. "Is that gun really necessary? What seems to be the problem?"

The skinny old woman hiked the butt of the gun onto her hip, but kept it trained on the dogs and Jessica in a distinctly unneighborly fashion. "Your dogs are wild beasts and need to be put down. Not only did a pack of them break down my fence, but one of my chickens is dead. My best layer. Never had problems like this when your grandparents owned the place."

"I'm sorry about your chicken." She kept her tone calm, as if she was talking to a nervous dog. "My fence is still intact," she pointed out. "My dogs didn't get onto your property. They didn't break your fence. And they didn't kill your chicken. Maybe a fox or coyote got inside your chicken coop."

"Don't you argue with me. Doris is dead. I already called Deputy Caldwell."

Jessica's nostrils flared with a sigh of relief, but for their own safety, she refused to relax or release the dogs from their stay position. "Good. Deputy Caldwell knows my dogs. He'll straighten this out." Garrett Caldwell was a captain in the Jackson County Sheriff's Office, in charge of the patrol division. He was not only in charge of local law enforcement in the county outside of the K C city limits, but he was practically a neighbor, living just off 40 Highway in the nearby town of Lone Jack. He was tough but fair, and the widower had become a friend. "He'll listen to the facts, assess the evidence. You'll get the answers you need, and my dogs will be safe."

Eloise glanced over her shoulder at the sound of a large vehicle crunching over gravel in the distance. "I expect that'll be him." She wheezed with the effort to keep the gun from pointing to the ground as she faced Jessica again. "You're in trouble now, missy."

Missy? Jessica wanted to laugh. She'd buried a husband and a child and felt as if she'd already lived the best part of her life. But she swallowed the dark humor as she watched the older woman wiggling her nose to work her glasses back up into place without letting go of the shotgun. Eloise Gardner was an octogenarian living a hard, lonely existence, trying to take care of things as best she could without the help, resources, or energy to fully manage on her own. "Miss Eloise, are you all right? Did you take your heart medication this morning?"

"Of course, I did." Eloise touched her age-spotted forehead as if trying to think. "I don't know. I'm not sure."

"Would you let me walk you back to your house?" Jessica offered. "We could check your pill box. I'd be happy to fix you a cup of tea and sit with you for a while." She glanced down at her faithful German shepherd mix. "I'd have to bring Shadow with me, but I promise, the other dogs will stay here."

"I..." For a moment, she looked as though she wanted to say yes to Jessica's offer. "No... Isla's coming today.

I gave her money for groceries." Suddenly, Eloise pulled her shoulders back with as much energy as her stooped posture allowed, raising the shotgun once more. "I don't want any of your dogs on my property. And who's fixing the latch on my chicken coop?"

"Miss Eloise?" A deep voice called out.

Jessica watched the tall man in his khaki uniform quietly striding up behind her neighbor. Garrett Caldwell stood a couple inches over six feet, and the protective vest he wore underneath his uniform made his sturdy chest and shoulders seem impossibly broad and imposing.

And then she saw Eloise Gardner swing around and point her shotgun straight at the deputy. "Garrett!"

Her warning proved unnecessary. In one swift, smooth movement, Garrett knocked the barrel of the shotgun aside, tugged it from her hands, and reached out to steady the old woman's arm to keep her from falling. Eloise yelped in surprise and clung to his forearm as he stepped behind her and braced her against his chest. All the while, he held the gun out with one strong arm and kept hold of Eloise until she stopped swaying.

The old woman's breathing fell back into a more normal rhythm, and Garrett released her and stepped back. "You all right, Miss Eloise?" Although she still seemed a little surprised by how quickly she'd been disarmed, she nodded. Then he turned his sharp green eyes across the fence to Jessica. "You okay?"

Jessica nodded, despite the lingering frissons of alarm that hummed through her veins. "Thank you, Deputy."

He touched the brim of his departmental ball cap, then concentrated on the white-haired lady beside him. "I'm not comfortable with you pointing a gun at me or anyone else when I haven't checked it out for myself." Garrett's tone held all the authority of his position, yet was surprisingly gentle with the frightened, angry, and possibly confused woman.

"It's not loaded. I just wanted to scare her. I don't feel safe around her dogs."

"All the same." He opened the shotgun, verified there were no rounds inside, then tucked the disabled weapon in the crook of his arm. "I want to make sure everyone is safe. Including you. This twelve-gauge seems a little too big for you to handle properly."

"It was my Hal's gun." Eloise sounded wistful at the mention of her late husband. "He took down an elk with it."

And she'd pointed that blunderbuss at her dogs? And her? And Garrett?

"I'm sure he did, ma'am. Now, what seems to be the problem?"

Eloise clutched Garrett's muscled forearm that was decorated with a faded black tattoo from his time in the military. "I want you to arrest this woman for siccing her dogs on my chickens."

Now that the imminent threat had been neutralized, he launched into investigator mode. "One of Jessie's dogs went after your chickens?"

"No," Jessica protested.

"Yes." The older woman's breathing was a little ragged. She pressed a gnarled hand against her heart.

"During the night. Of course, I didn't hear it, but one of those mutts chewed through the latch on my coop and the hens got out. This morning, there were hardly any eggs when I went to gather them, so I know something upset them. I found Doris dead by the side of the highway. She was my best layer." Even though she was shorter by a few inches, the white-haired woman managed to look down her nose at Jessica. "Your dogs chased her right out into the road."

"My dogs haven't left my property," Jessica insisted. Then she dropped her voice to a whisper she hoped only Garrett could hear. "Although, they did go off about two o'clock this morning. I never saw anything. Maybe she had an intruder, and that's what they heard."

His lips barely moved as he answered in an equally hushed tone. "I think she needs to relax and put her feet up for a bit. She looks pale and sounds winded."

"I asked if she took her medications this morning. She couldn't remember."

"She's upset about her damn chicken."

"Not. My. Dogs."

Garrett arched a brow over one moss-colored eye, silently asking her to give up the argument. Then he smiled at the older woman and spoke in his full, deeply pitched voice. "Are the rest of your chickens okay, ma'am?"

After several moments, Eloise nodded. "They were all inside the fence this morning, but the latch is broken. Someone braced it shut with a rock."

"Well, my dogs didn't do that."

"Jessie." Garrett's eyes narrowed, asking her to be

the more magnanimous complainant here. Once she nodded, he turned back to the older woman. "Miss Eloise, you go back to your house. I'll meet you there in a few minutes to take your statement and return the gun. I'll look around to make sure everything is secure."

"Thank you." Once the white-haired woman had taken a few steps toward her house, Garrett crossed to the fence. After a quick inspection of the broken railing, he braced one hand on a sturdier post and swung his legs up over both fences onto her property.

The moment he dropped down onto the grass, Shadow raised his head and growled. Rex yawned, growing bored with staying in one place. Toby's tail was wagging hard enough to kick up a cloud of dirt and dry grass on the ground behind him, but even the friendly Lab who'd greeted Garrett on more than one occasion eyed Jessica's hand and maintained his stay position.

Garrett froze in place, and Eloise hurried back to the fence in a huff. "You see, Deputy? Those dogs are a threat to all of us."

"No, they're not." Jessica was tired of defending herself and the work she was doing here. She latched on to Garrett's gaze and willed him to side with her. "These are three of my best students. None of them are smarter than Shadow. They know the property lines, and that they aren't to cross them without me. They guard *my* land. They don't invade hers. They're all well-fed and have plenty of stimulation. They don't need to be stealing chickens for breakfast or chasing them for entertainment."

Garrett nodded toward Shadow. "If these dogs are so well trained, why is that one growling at me?"

"Because you're holding that gun. You're half a foot taller than me and you look like a threat." She glanced at her outstretched hand, still holding her dogs in place. "But he won't go after you unless I give the command."

"The fence is broken, Jessie." Making the concession to Shadow's watchful eye, Garrett laid Eloise's open shotgun on the ground behind him. He visibly relaxed his posture, although he didn't move any closer. "Your smaller dogs might not be able to get out. But one of these three could."

"Are you going to call them off?" Eloise prodded, seeming more energized now that backup had arrived.

"Are you going to accuse my dogs of something they didn't do?"

"Jessie." Garrett exhaled a weary breath, drawing her attention to the silver-studded beard stubble shading his jaw. Standing closer, she realized the lines beside his mouth were etched more deeply than the last time she'd seen him.

"Garrett?" Something locked up deep inside her fluttered with concern. Maybe the same impulse that had her worried about Eloise's health. Garrett looked exhausted. Had he worked the night shift? Had he even slept? Who looked out for the strong boss man when he had a rough night? Apparently, it wasn't a job he did for himself. "Are you all right?"

He let out his breath on a slow, weary exhale, but didn't answer. Whatever fatigue she'd detected didn't stop him from smiling at her neighbor and speaking in a tone that commanded authority, even as his words offered compassion and reassurance. "Miss Eloise, go back to the house and fix yourself a cup of tea or a shot of whiskey to calm your nerves. I'll be over in a few minutes to return your shotgun and take a closer look at what happened."

"All right. I could do with a few minutes to myself." The older woman smiled. "With Doris's demise, I guess I'll be making fried chicken for dinner. Deputy, if you'd like to join me. Isla will be here. She'd love to see you." The older woman pushed her glasses up on the bridge of her nose and winked.

"Your granddaughter?" Jessica thought she detected a ruddy hue to Garrett's carved cheekbones and held back a smirk at his embarrassment. "She's a mite young for me, ma'am."

"Nonsense. She's thirty. Just broke up with her latest boyfriend. I told her he was no good. Out drinking nearly every night. Probably doing drugs."

"Isla or the boyfriend?"

Eloise bristled at the question. "I'm just telling you she's available."

"I appreciate you thinking of me, ma'am. But I'm not interested. I'm just here to do my job."

Eloise propped her hands on her hips. "You've been widowed for ten years, Garrett Caldwell. It's time you got laid again."

There was definitely a blush now. Jessica curled her lips between her teeth to hide her grin at Eloise's blatant matchmaking attempt. Just because the man had lost his wife to cancer a decade earlier didn't mean he hadn't dated or been with a woman since then. Garrett Caldwell was a catch. If you had a thing for silver foxes with a sense of humor and muscles to spare. She doubted if he needed Eloise Gardner's or anyone's help if he wanted to get laid.

Of course, Jessica hadn't slept with a man since losing Jonathan twelve years ago. Being abstinent for that long, she was practically a dinosaur, or at least an old maid. Dogs, friends, and more often than not, loneliness were her companions. But it was a choice she'd made. Whatever decisions Garrett had made about his love life, it wasn't her business. Nor was it Eloise Gardner's.

But Garrett had the situation well in hand. He pointed to the chicken coop and house beyond. "Go home, Eloise. And don't you be aiming a gun at your neighbor or her dogs again, you hear me?"

"Yes, sir." She turned and headed back to her house, her steps much lighter than a woman in her eighties ought to be. "Oh, I like a man who gets bossy and says what he means. Just like my Hal used to…"

Once the older woman was out of earshot, Garrett cursed a single word, then faced Jessica again. "I wouldn't put it past Miss Eloise to wring the neck of that chicken herself and call my office as an excuse to get me out here. She's lonesome, her granddaughter's horny, and quite frankly, I feel safer on this side of the property line than I do on hers. Now, please call off your dogs, so we can talk."

"You poor man." Jessica barely masked her grin as she released the dogs. Toby and Rex scampered away to find their next adventure, but Shadow thrust his head into her hand, demanding pats, and remained by her side. "Terrorized by a lonely eighty-five-year-old woman with arthritis and heart issues. Need me to rescue you?"

He scrubbed his palm over the stubble of his jaw, and she was struck once again by how tired he looked. Okay. Not in the mood for teasing.

"I'm sorry, Garrett," she apologized. "Clearly, you're here on business. Thank you for alleviating the threat and not forcing me to lock up my dogs. Looks like it's already been a long morning for you. May I offer you a cup of coffee?"

"It's been a long twenty-four hours," he admitted. "I've already had too much coffee. Besides—" he grinned, and she pretended she didn't find this boyish, charming side of Garrett Caldwell as attractive as she did his scruffy workaholic look "—I've got a caramel macchiato for you out in my truck."

So, they *were* doing the teasing thing, after all. Jessica smiled. Apparently, he'd stopped at the coffee shop in town. Occasionally, she'd met him there when their schedules allowed, and he knew her weakness. "Are you trying to bribe me?"

"If I have to. I'm asking for your help."

"Oh." The seriousness of his tone ended the friendly banter they usually shared before it ever got started. "Did you or one of your team pick up another stray? Is the shelter full?" She'd helped the sheriff's department several times in the past, rounding up strays and housing them for a few days until she found a safe shelter where they could be housed in Kansas City or one of the nearby small towns—if she didn't have the time or space to take on a new project herself. "I've got a client here right now I need to finish with, but I can drive into Lone Jack after that if you need me."

"I've got human problems this time."

Jessica tilted her gaze up to Garrett's, analyzing what had stamped his handsome features with such fatigue. The mask of charm he'd used with Eloise had vanished. "Did you sleep at all last night? Are you working a case?"

Instead of answering her questions, he asked her one. "Are you pressing charges against Eloise? She did threaten you with a gun—even if it wasn't loaded."

"No. I know she's had a hard time of it since her husband died. I knew her daughter, Misty—Isla's mother—from spending summers here with Gran and Papa. But I haven't seen her once in the three years since I moved here and started transforming the property from a working farm into a rescue operation and training center."

"Yeah, Misty followed a man to Montana—or maybe it was Wyoming. Eloise doesn't talk about her. I don't think that was an amicable parting." Garrett shrugged. "Isla's no help. She can't keep a job or a man. And I know for a fact that Isla's ex-husband, and at least one of the men I've seen her hanging with at the bar in town, have rap sheets. Drugs. Drunk and Disorderlies. Burglary and theft."

"Wow." Jessica hadn't realized just how dangerous some of the people in Eloise Gardner's world could be. "No wonder her reaction was to call you and protect herself with a gun. Do you think either of those men, or even Isla, are a threat to her? I know she has some money from her husband's life insurance. She has the spirit of a cantankerous old woman, but she's fragile."

"I know. It worries me, too." Garrett tugged off his ball cap and combed his fingers through the salt-and-pepper spikes of his short hair, leaving a rumpled mess in their wake. Jessica curled her fingers into her palms, surprised by the urge to smooth it back into place. She and Garrett were friends, nothing more. Occasional coworkers who shared a love for caffeine and canines. A widow and a widower who were perfectly content to live out their days without the stress and complications of forging a new relationship. "I was half hoping she was fending off Isla's boyfriend with her shotgun instead of you. I need something to explain the weird things happening around here."

"Weird?" Jessica's hand instinctively moved to Shadow's warm fur. "What do you mean?"

Garrett settled his cap back on top of his head. "The reason I got here so quickly was because I was checking out a vandalism call at the Russells' summer cabin. Someone cut a screen and broke a window. Rifled through the medicine cabinet. Looks like they might have stolen a couple of small items. Didn't touch the TV, though. Probably couldn't get it out through the window."

Jessica drifted half a step closer to Garrett, her body subconsciously responding to the concern she felt for him, even though her brain wouldn't allow her to touch him. "On the other side of the Gardner farm? You think that's related to the dead chicken and broken fence?"

"I don't know. But I don't like a mystery. Too many little incidents like this start adding up, and they become something big. *Something big* is the call I don't want to answer."

Had he been working these *little incidents* all night? She wasn't naive enough to think she'd left serious crime behind her in Kansas City. But Garrett's suspicions made her nervous that something more dangerous than a frightened old woman and a spate of vandalism might be lurking in the hills, forests and farmland around her. "What do you think is going on?"

"Could be vagrants looking for food or a place to sleep. The weather is warming up and we've had a few hitchhikers out on the highway trying to leave the city. Could be bored teenagers entertaining themselves by causing trouble." He shook his head, clearly frustrated by his lack of answers. "My gut tells me it's something bigger. Maybe these petty crimes are a distraction to keep me and my officers busy with calls, so we don't see a bigger threat happening. Someone could be casing the area to plan a bigger score, or they're setting up a drug trafficking route, or they're clearing a path to move stolen goods in or out of Kansas City." He pulled off his cap again and scrubbed his fingers through his short hair. "I just pray there's not something I'm missing because I've lost a few hours of sleep."

This time Jessica did reach for him. She wound her fingers around his wrist and pulled his hand from his hair, stilling the rough outlet for his frustration. His muscles tensed beneath her touch, and she quickly pulled away from the heat of his skin that singed her fingertips. But she didn't back away from her support. "Garrett, you've been with the sheriff's department for twenty-some years. You're captain of your own division." Even without the badge on his chest and the extra bars on his collar, the man exuded wisdom and experience—and the ability to get the job done. "You'll figure it out."

"I don't want anyone taking advantage of that old woman out here by herself. Or you." He glanced back at Mrs. Gardner's place, where he'd parked his truck. "In fact, I brought the coffee as an excuse to get you to sit down and talk to me about Soren Hauck. He and a buddy of his skipped a couple of days of school this week."

"You don't have to bribe me to have a conversation." Jessica considered the teenager who worked for her two evenings a week and on Saturdays. She'd convinced him to pull his long reddish-brown hair back into a ponytail for safety reasons, but wished he'd trade his fancy high-top athletic shoes for a pair of solid work boots. But if he didn't mind getting them dirty, she couldn't really complain. "I don't know if I can tell you anything. I haven't had any issue with Soren not showing up for work. He's good with my dogs. But he's only part-time. I don't see him every day like I do his grandfather." Hugo Hauck had once farmed the land on the other side of Jessica's property. But now that his son—Soren's father—had taken over, the retired farmer had hired on as her part-time handyman, milking her female goat for her each morning and keeping the facilities running smoothly. "Hugo has worked for me since almost the beginning. He's the one who asked if I could take his grandson on part-time when he turned sixteen. Soren got his own car and needs gas money. Plus, whatever else teenage boys need."

Garrett nodded, probably expecting an answer like that. "I wish I could get Miss Eloise to take as much interest in Hugo Hauck as she does in me."

Jessica couldn't help the chuckle that escaped. "Matchmaking, Deputy Caldwell?"

"Trying to get her to focus on any other man besides me. Just because I'm single, it doesn't mean I'm available."

Not available? The most interesting man she'd met since her own husband had died was off the market? Jessica silently cursed the flash of disappointment she felt at his pronouncement. Garrett Caldwell was seasoned like a fine wine. He was fit and masculine, unafraid to take charge and be the boss. She'd learned to be strong and independent since her husband's murder twelve years earlier. And while she was compassionate and patient with clients and neighbors, she didn't suffer fools or cheats or charmers who had no substance to back up their clever words. Garrett Caldwell was all about substance. She might be attracted to a man who could go toe to toe with her, but that didn't mean she wanted to lay claim to one. She needed a friend more than she needed a lover. The county needed a deputy and protector more than she needed a mate. Still, that lonesome kernel of feminine longing that wished for the life she'd lost asked, "Are you seeing someone?"

Garrett held her gaze for several moments. But just

when her lips parted to question the intensity of that stare, he answered. "No. But when I do get involved with a woman, it won't be Isla Gardner."

Why did that sound like a promise? And why did all that unabashed male intensity focused on her make her breath stutter in her chest? Resolutely shaking off the little frissons of interest that made her uncomfortable with the personal turn to their conversation, Jessica brushed a strand of hair off her face and tucked it into the base of her ponytail at the back of her head. "Get things settled with Miss Eloise, while I finish up with my client." She thumbed over her shoulder as she backed toward the trees. "I'll meet you on my front porch in about twenty minutes."

He touched the brim of his cap and turned to the fence to pick up the gun. "It's a date."

His words made her realize that touching him and laughing with him and thinking about his sex life had blurred the line of friendship she wanted to keep between them. She needed to get back to her comfort zone. "Not a date, Garrett. We're two friends of a certain age who like to share a cup of morning coffee."

"A certain age?" He grunted at the terminology. "How old do you think I am?"

"Old enough to turn Miss Eloise's head, apparently," she teased. Because friends teased each other.

"You're only four years younger than me, Jessie. So, you watch who you're calling old," he taunted right back. "I think I've got a lot of good years left, even if you don't."

"You sure know how to flatter a girl."

Something snapped inside her head, and the present blurred into the past.

"You sure know how to flatter a girl." Jessica pouted and tugged her hand from her husband's. *"I'm eight months pregnant with the seed you planted there, big fella. Saying goodbye to me and my 'big baby belly' makes me sound like a beached whale."*

John stopped in the foyer and turned, leaning in to press his lips against that pout. He kissed the tension from her mouth and kept kissing her until her fingers were curling into the lapels of his suit and she was stretching up on her toes to drink in the love and passion of his plundering lips.

When he ended the kiss and she sank back onto her heels, they were both slightly breathless. "What I meant to say was goodbye, my love. Have a good day at work. And..." He knelt in front of her, gently cradling her distended belly and pressing a kiss to the visible tremors they could see at the front of her dress where the baby was kicking. "Goodbye to the strong boy my lovely wife is carrying so beautifully for us."

Jessica cradled the back of John's head and smiled in utter contentment as he crooned love words to the infant she carried. "Much better, Counselor."

John was smiling as he picked up his briefcase and reached for the front door. "Remember to stay off your feet as much as you can today. You're in the office all day, right?" When she nodded, he pressed one last kiss to her lips. "I'll pick up some lunch for us when I'm done with this morning's hearings. Noon work for you?"

"Sounds perfect." He pulled the door open, and Jessica followed to catch it. "I'll see you..."

John had stopped. "What are you...?"

He shoved her back inside at the same time she saw the rumpled, wild-eyed man pointing a gun at John's head.

"You took everything from me! You lousy divorce lawyer!"

The explosion of the gunshot jolted through her.

Zeus heard the commotion and charged from the kitchen, barking a vicious warning.

Something warm and sticky splattered on her face. John crumpled to the porch.

Then the wild-eyed man's eyes met hers.

Run.

"Jessie!"

Strong hands clasped her shoulders and she startled, shaking off the unfamiliar touch.

"Easy. I've got you." A man's face swam in front of hers, and she put up her hands to ward him off. Until his green eyes came into focus, and she read the concern there.

John's eyes were blue.

The wild eyes were brown.

"Garrett?" She patted him on the chest, obliquely wondering why it was so hard. She breathed in deeply, silently cursing the cruel tricks her mind could play on her, even after all this time. "I'm okay." She took another breath, then another, pulling herself squarely back into the present. Then she felt a warm paw pressing against her thigh, and she collapsed to the ground to wrap her arms around Shadow's neck and bury her nose in his fur. "I'm okay. Mama's okay. You haven't had to do that for a while, have you, boy. Good Shadow."

"Good boy." Garrett went down on one knee in front of her, running his hand along Shadow's back, comforting the dog when Jessica wouldn't let him comfort her. "Where'd you go? I said your name three times."

"Sorry."

"Don't apologize." Garrett pulled back as she embraced her dog. "The flashbacks suck, don't they?"

"I haven't had one in a long time. But they're still there, every now and then." She forced her nose out of Shadow's fur and looked at Garrett. "You have post-traumatic stress, too?"

"I wasn't a choirboy in the Army." His face creased with a wry smile that never reached his eyes. "A good ol' country boy like me who grew up hunting? I was a sniper."

Jessica's stomach clenched, imagining the violence he must have dealt with fighting a war. "I'm sorry, Garrett. You must have seen some awful things. Done some things you aren't even allowed to talk about."

"It was a while ago. I've talked to a therapist. The military is getting better about helping their soldiers cope with what we have to deal with." He threaded his fingers into Shadow's fur again, and the dog lay down, now panting contentedly between them. "What about you?"

"Talk to a therapist?" She nodded. "She was the one who recommended I get a dog ten years ago. So, I wouldn't be alone on the nights I couldn't sleep, when the memories tried to take over."

"Shadow's your lifeline," Garrett speculated.

She smiled at her beloved companion. "I didn't initially train him to put his paw on me to wake me up or pull me back to the present. But he was a natural. Dogs are so empathetic. They pick up on emotions—happiness, excitement, anger, distress."

"And your success with Shadow inspired you to start K-9 Ranch—to rescue dogs and help others who need a friend."

Jessica could feel her heart rate slowing down, the nightmare receding and her thoughts clearing. Part of her recovery was due to Shadow's warmth and support, but she suspected part of her ability to breathe more easily was due to Garrett's calm, deep-pitched voice and the quiet conversation they were sharing. "Gave me a purpose. A reason to stop grieving around the clock and get up in the morning."

"Do you know what set it off this time?" he asked.

Uh-uh. Now that she had the nightmare under control, she wasn't dredging it up again. How did she explain the perfect storm of Eloise's gun, the feelings for Garrett she refused to acknowledge, and the innocent phrase that had been some of the last words she'd spoken to her husband, anyway? Jessica pushed to her feet. "You'd better go. I don't want Eloise on my front step like Almira Gulch with a basket trying to take Toto away from Dorothy."

Garrett straightened as well, his shoulders blocking

the morning sun, he was standing so close. "Are you all right? Should I call someone?"

"There's no one to call." Shadow stood beside her, leaning against her leg so that she could continue to stroke the warmth of his head "I have everything I need right here."

"You can call *me*. Anytime."

"You're not on duty 24/7."

He reached down to scratch around Shadow's ears, but angled his gaze up to hers. "No. But I am your friend 24/7. Call whenever you need me."

Jessica covered his hand where it rested on Shadow's shoulder. "Only if you promise to do the same. Like when you pull an all-nighter and need a break from interviewing victims and suspects, and analyzing crime scenes." She quickly stepped away the moment she felt her body's desire to move *toward* him. "I need to get back to my client, Mollie. Right now, she's afraid of everything and everybody. Including the dog she wants to adopt."

Garrett inhaled a deep breath, his posture and tone shifting into deputy mode. "Afraid? Anything I need to know about?"

Like he needed to take one more burden onto his broad shoulders this morning. Besides, she truly hadn't seen any evidence of a threat to Mollie beyond the woman's own skittish behavior. Jessica shrugged. "She drives out from Kansas City. Divorced from an abusive ex. As far as I know, she dumped him and she's trying to move on with her life."

"Does her situation trigger you?"

"No. My husband was never violent with me. John was a good man."

"She have a restraining order out on him?"

Jessica nodded. "Mollie showed me his picture. But I've never seen him in person. If I find out anything that's concerning, I'll let you know. Otherwise, I want her to trust in me. And in Magnus."

"The deaf dog?"

She was much more comfortable talking about work. "Only in one ear. He makes up for it with the other. And killer eyesight. I'm teaching them to rely on hand signals more than verbal commands. But it's a process."

Garrett crossed back to the fence to retrieve the empty shotgun. "Maybe I will run prints on this fence and the chicken coop, see if I can get a match to the break-in at the Russells' cabin. Just to rule out a trespasser who might be following your client. Let me know if whoever is scaring her shows up out here. Lock yourself and Mollie in the house with the dogs if you see her ex. Stay away from the windows and call me."

"I will."

He glanced back across the fence. "Wish me luck. If Isla is there already, I may be calling for backup."

Jessica appreciated that he could make her laugh, especially after her mini meltdown. She suspected the man could handle himself in any situation. But he was too much of a gentleman to be downright cruel to her needy neighbor. "Good luck. Figure out your mystery. Then bring me my caramelly coffee, and we'll talk more about Soren."

He paused with one hand on the fence's top railing. "You're sure you're okay?"

"I will be."

He touched the brim of his cap, then vaulted over the fence again.

Jessica watched him stride away. The man had a nice ass to go along with those broad shoulders. And he always got her coffee order right when he stopped by the ranch.

She could see why the Gardner ladies had the hots for him.

And why she had to keep her guard up around his take-charge strength and surprisingly gentle compassion. She couldn't do a relationship again. Not even with a good man like Garrett. She'd had love. She'd been growing her family. She'd planned a future. And every last bit of it had been violently taken from her.

She was a survivor.

She could live her life. Be useful. Find joy and a purpose with her dogs.

But she wasn't strong enough to love and lose again.

Chapter Three

"Come on, Shadow." Jessica patted the rangy dog's flank and headed through the trees back to the house.

She needed to think about why the flashback had hit her in the middle of her conversation with Garrett. She'd been doing so well for such a long time that it was disconcerting to find out how her mind could unexpectedly and painfully snap her back to the past. She was supposed to be fine on her own. She *was* fine on her own. She had coping skills that should have defused the waking nightmare long before it sucked her in. Instead, she'd been blindsided by the memories, and now she felt raw and vulnerable.

And worse, Garrett, a man she called her friend and whom she admired, had seen her lose it.

She needed to clear her head and focus on something else, so that she could look at the situation objectively and come up with a plan to identify the trigger and neutralize its effect on her. She thought she'd gotten past the sight of a gun triggering her PTSD, and certainly, once Garrett confirmed the shotgun wasn't loaded, she hadn't viewed Eloise as a threat. An annoyance, maybe—someone she worried about—but not a threat. And, of course, she'd uttered the same phrase to Garrett that she had to John all those years ago, just before his client's ex had ended his life. There had to be something more working on her. Was there something pricking at her subconscious? Some detail in her life that her eyes missed, but her mind was subtly aware of? Was there something about her world she wasn't able to control? It had been a few years since she'd had regular sessions with her therapist. Maybe it was time to give her a call to do a follow-up wellness check, just to make sure she wasn't regressing.

With that much of a plan in mind, she crossed the driveway that led up to the house. Walking past the kennels and training corral, Jessica petted the dogs who ran up to her, looking for Mollie and Magnus. "Mollie?"

Soren was at school—at least he should be—and Hugo would have already shooed the goats out into their pasture and was probably running errands since she didn't see his truck parked in its usual spot beside the barn. Maybe she should offer Hugo's services to Eloise. See if her neighbors could distract each other long enough to get them out of Garrett's hair and create a peaceful coexistence for her, as well. She'd offer to pay him to repair Eloise's fence and chicken coop.

"Jessica?" The dark-haired woman hurried out of the barn. Magnus jogged along beside her, a faded red KONG wedged squarely in his jaw. Good. Mollie had taken her advice and had been playing with her dog. "I didn't know whether to come and find you or wait until you got back."

"Why?" Worried that the young woman's flushed

cheeks meant something more than running around in the fresh air with her dog, she reached out and squeezed Mollie's hand. "Is something wrong?"

Mollie tugged her into step beside her. "I think you've had a break-in."

"What?" Three properties in a row that had all had some kind of trespasser? What was going on around here? "Show me."

Jessica moved ahead of Mollie into the cooler air of the barn. Other than the goats, who stayed inside each night, and a box secluded in a stall where an Australian shepherd stray had given birth to a litter of mixed-breed puppies a few weeks ago, the barn was used for storage and a sheltered training facility when the weather outside wasn't ideal. Under her direction, Hugo and his grandson had enclosed two of the stalls and added a concrete floor to secure Hugo's tools and have a place to store the donations of food and supplies she often received.

The Australian shepherd raised her head when the women walked past with Shadow and Magnus. "Hey, mama. You okay?" Some of the straw in their stall had been squashed, though that could just have been Hugo taking in fresh food and water for the dog. A quick check showed they were all safe. The pups were either nursing or sleeping. "Good girl."

Walking to the far end of the barn, Jessica could see the damage that had been done. The door to the first storage room was shut tight, with the padlock secured through the latch. But the door to the second storage room stood slightly ajar. The padlock was still secured through its steel loop. But the hinge that secured the latch to the doorframe was bent and hanging by a single screw, and there were gouges in the wood around the lock, as if someone had taken a rock or hammer to it when they couldn't get the padlock open.

"It was like this when you came in?" Jessica asked.

"Not exactly," Mollie answered. "I unlocked this room to get Magnus's toy." She touched the first door. "But as soon as he realized this was where his KONG was stored, he got excited. He jumped up and scratched at the wood. He must have jostled the frame. The latch fell off, and the door drifted open. Then I saw the mess inside."

"It looks as though someone tried to make it look like it hadn't been disturbed. But he lacked either the tools or the time to do so."

"I didn't touch anything. I know the police don't like it when you do. In case you want to report it." Mollie pointed to the barn's open archway. "I took Magnus outside to play so that he wouldn't accidentally do more damage and waited for you to take a look at it."

"Good thinking." Jessica put the dogs into a stay and told Mollie to keep hold of Magnus's leash. Then she pulled her sleeve down over her fingers and nudged the door open.

A creepy sense of violation ran its chilly fingers down her spine as she surveyed the room. Everything was askew on one of the metal shelves inside, as if some critter had run along the back and knocked things out of place. A glass mason jar where she stored treats lay shattered on the floor. And while she was certain it had been full, most of the treats were gone. She spotted a torn bag of dog food with kibble spilling out. Old blankets that had once been neatly stacked were now piled haphazardly on the floor. There was a depression in the middle, as though the careless critter had made a nest there. And one of the blankets—probably the oldest and rattiest one of all—was missing. Who would steal a holey blanket but leave the old radio/CD player on the worktable untouched? She supposed a possum or rat could have gotten in by crawling through a gap in the siding below the barn's outer wall. It wouldn't be the first time a wild animal had helped itself to her supply of dog food. A raccoon would have the dexterity to pad its nest with the blankets, but that explanation didn't quite make sense, either.

Jessica made several quick mental notes of all that was damaged or missing before backing out. She shooed the curious dogs away from the door and reached for the cell phone in her back pocket. She bypassed calling 9-1-1 and pulled up the number of the man she knew was already working the case.

Jessica hated to dump anything more on Garrett Caldwell's plate today. But she had a feeling he'd want to know that her place had been included in his weird crime spree.

First, a busted fence abutting her land, and now a broken hinge and a ransacked storage room? Someone seemed to be making their way through all the properties south of 40 Highway, heading east out of the city. There was definitely a spate of petty crimes moving through the county. Although, unless she counted the chicken, there was no murder, assault or other violent crime. Was Garrett right? Maybe Soren and his truant friend had been messing around last night. Could all these little incidents be indicative of something sinister going on? Were they a prelude to something more threatening about to happen?

"Deputy Caldwell." Even as she felt guilty about reporting yet another incident of vandalism, Jessica warmed to the sound of his voice, and the wary trepidation she felt eased to a manageable level. He must have recognized her number or name on his phone. "Jessie?"

"Are you still coming over?"

"I'm headed to my truck now."

"Good. I have something to show you."

She heard his weary sigh. "Why don't I think that means you baked a batch of your peanut butter cookies to go with our coffee?"

"Sorry. Your mystery just expanded into my barn."

His powerful truck engine roared to life in the background. "I'm on my way."

Jessica tucked her phone back into her pocket. She wanted these break-ins solved, too, now that it had come to her K-9 Ranch. Even without Garrett's instincts and experience to suggest it, she had a feeling there was something bigger and more threatening lurking in the fringes of her world.

Twelve years ago, she hadn't known just how dangerous the world could be. Now she couldn't help but think the worst.

She wanted to believe that whatever had gotten

into the storage room and made that little nest wasn't human.

But only a human would need to break the lock to get inside.

GARRETT HAD NEVER been so glad to get a phone call reporting a break-in in his whole career. Jessie's message was the excuse he needed to finally extricate himself from Eloise Gardner's machinations and enlist one of his officers to take over for him at the Gardner farm.

Eloise had indeed forgotten her heart medications that morning, so he'd sat at the kitchen table with her and watched her take the pills and check her blood pressure before jotting down notes about her morning. A quick inspection of her chicken coop revealed that nothing had chewed through anything. Yes, the gate to the yard had been forced open, and there was evidence that the chickens had scattered, then been chased back in—minus Doris, of course.

But the gate had been tied shut with a chunk of faded red yarn. Garrett knew Jessie had trained her dogs to do a number of amazing things. But not one of them had grown opposable thumbs and the ability to tie a knot.

Isla seemed to have forgotten the grocery list Eloise had given her, and when Eloise told him she'd given Isla her debit card to purchase the groceries, Garrett had immediately called to make sure she wasn't spending her grandmother's money on clothes or partying or her latest boyfriend. His instincts had proved to be sadly accurate when he heard a man's voice yelling at Isla to get off the phone and get her butt out of the car to get the cash they needed from the ATM. Not that the conversation he'd overheard was proof enough to stand up in court—maybe they were using cash for the groceries. But it was reason enough to dispatch a second officer to the bank to get a better idea of what might be going on. At least, he could get a possible ID on the shady boyfriend. Taking advantage of an elderly citizen was one of Garrett's pet peeves, and something he was always willing to investigate.

But he had a bigger case he needed to focus on right now. And he could guarantee that Officer Maya Hernandez wouldn't have to fend off Eloise's repeated attempts to get a man to stay for dinner and married off to her granddaughter.

Plus, he was worried by Jessie's news that something odd had happened at her place, too, last night.

Garrett dashed out to his truck and started the engine. He barely resisted turning on the lights and siren. He raised his hand in a quick wave to Officer Hernandez as he barreled past her down Eloise's gravel drive.

Jessie needed him. And, even if it was just the badge she needed right now, that spoke to every protective male instinct in him. That was the problem. Jessie Bennington was stubborn and independent in a way his Hayley had never been. In the years since they'd met over a call to round up a stray that had gotten trapped in a condemned building, he'd learned that Jessie was smart and funny and caring. But the moment things seemed to get too personal, she threw up walls and attitude as if she had something raw and vulnerable inside that she needed to protect.

The hell of it was that, after witnessing her panic attack this morning, he suspected she was protecting herself from something horrific. He wanted in behind those walls so that he could help keep her safe from whatever that horror might be.

Garrett understood that she didn't want to be taken care of. His late wife, Hayley, had been sick with cancer on and off for so long that it had become second nature to be more caretaker and companion than equal partner or certainly lover. It had been his honor and duty to leave the Army and be there for the woman who had owned his heart since they'd been high school sweethearts. But it had also been emotionally exhausting. He'd grieved, thrown himself into his work, first on the department's special teams unit, and then as a senior deputy. Eventually he'd been ready to move on, had given dating a few tries, and run into more Isla Gardners than anyone he'd actually consider diving into a long-term relationship with.

Then Jessica Bennington inherited her grandparents' farm and had become part of his world.

Jessie had shown him how attractive a different kind of woman could be. Mature sensibilities. Strong. Driven. Funny. Sexy without even trying with that long gorgeous silvery-blond hair and trim figure. He wanted to mean something to her. She might not need or want a caretaker, but she could certainly use a partner, couldn't she? Yet, waiting for her to reach the same decision he had already reached required the patience of a saint. Garrett liked to think of himself as one of the good guys, but he was no saint.

Whether or not she ever decided to give him a shot, or clung tightly to her friends-only rule, he'd worry about her anyway. He knew a little about her past—her husband had been killed in a home invasion, and she'd been wounded. Certainly, that was trauma enough to stick with anyone. But he hadn't witnessed her have a flashback before. The sheer terror in her pale features had made him want to wrap her up in his arms and carry her far away from whatever nightmare had seized her.

If whatever she wanted him to see on her property had triggered even an nth of the fear he'd witnessed this morning, he was going to go alpha male on somebody's ass. And probably pay the price when Jessie told him to back off and do his job—that she didn't need or want a protector to rescue her.

Caring about Jessie Bennington was an exercise in patience and frustration.

Deep breaths, Caldwell. He mentally calmed himself the same way he had before making a kill shot or taking down a perp like he had during his years as a sniper. Tamping down his emotions and slipping on the mantle of Deputy Garrett Caldwell, he slowed his truck and rolled up to Jessie's house without spitting up too much gravel.

Jessie waved to him from the barn, and he climbed down from his truck and strode toward her and the woman with curly dark hair standing beside her. The younger woman had a white-knuckled grip around the leash hooked up to the Belgian Malinois sitting beside her.

Garrett shortened his stride and slowed his pace. Jes-

sie's client must have a thing about men in uniform—
or men, period. He recognized the nervous look of an
abused woman and wondered who had put that wari-
ness in her eyes. She was another rescue project of
Jessie's, no doubt. He did what he could to help ease
the young woman's anxiety by moving closer to Jessie and taking off his cap to make a polite introduc-
tion. He scrubbed his fingers through his spiky hair,
suspecting he was making more of a mess rather than
straightening his appearance. "Jessie." She nodded in
greeting. "You've had a break-in here, too?"

"Mollie discovered it. She volunteered to stay in
case you have any questions for her." That had been
a big ask, judging by the woman's reluctance to make
eye contact with him. "This is Garrett Caldwell. Mollie Crane," she introduced. "He's a friend as well as
a captain in the sheriff's department. You can trust
him. I do."

Friend. Trust.

He was grateful for Jessie's words and vowed to
make sure he lived up to that faith in him. Anything
else between them could come later—if she ever gave
him the chance. Garrett extended his hand. "Ms. Crane.
Nice to meet you. Sorry it's under these circumstances."

Slowly, the woman brought her hand up to lightly
grasp his. "Nice to meet you, Deputy Caldwell."

Garrett smiled and quickly released her hand. "You
want to show me what you found?"

"Magnus. Heel." Mollie tugged the flop-eared dog
to his feet and led them into the barn. Garrett couldn't
help but notice that she kept one hand on the dog's short

fur, just like he'd often seen Jessie reach for Shadow. The dog was an anchor. A comfort. Something to focus on besides whatever trauma she was dealing with inside her head.

What Mollie Crane lacked in confidence, she more than made up for with impeccable manners and an eye for detail. Thirty minutes later, she and Magnus were driving back to Kansas City, and Garrett had a thorough report from the two women, detailing the mess in the storage room and the suspected items that were missing, including a blanket, kibble, and some dog treats.

Not exactly a million-dollar crime spree. But something weird was going on in his part of Jackson County.

By the time Garrett had snapped a few pictures with his phone, Hugo Hauck had returned, and between the three of them, they got the storage area cleaned up and had reattached the hinge, so that the door would close. While they worked, Garrett asked Hugo a few casual questions about Soren. The old man praised his grandson for his affinity in working with the dogs, but he also complained that the teen had made some new friends, and Hugo caught them drinking beer out in one of the pastures one night. He even went so far as to say that he'd smelled pot on the boy's clothing, and that his parents had laid down the law about taking away his car and other privileges if he went any further down that road.

Garrett wanted to talk to Soren himself, get a feeling if the disciplinary consequences had been enough to scare him away from his experimental behavior—or if he and his friends had simply gone underground and gotten sneakier about their vices. Maybe by breaking into a deserted cabin to party? Or engaging in other criminal mischief while under the influence of drugs or alcohol?

It was after twelve by the time Hugo left to go home and Garrett walked Jessie back to her house. Shadow ambled up the porch steps ahead of them and curled up on the cushions of the teakwood bench near the front door.

"I'm afraid your coffee is another casualty of this morning's events. It's ice-cold by now," he apologized. He stopped on the sidewalk as Jessie climbed the front steps, ostensibly because he needed to get back to the office to type up his reports and check in on his staff— but also because he enjoyed watching Jessie's backside in the worn, fitted jeans that hugged her curves. He was due one good thing today, wasn't he? He'd had a hell of a long shift since reporting for duty yesterday morning and working through the night. He wasn't being pervy about it. Just taking note of something that gave him pleasure, and then he'd be on his way. "I need to get preliminary reports written up on all these incidents. Maybe I'll find a thread that connects them. Then, hopefully, I can take off early and get a decent night's sleep tonight." Possibly feeling ignored that he'd mentioned shut-eye instead of a meal, his stomach grumbled loudly enough that Shadow raised his head at the noise. He chuckled as he patted his flat belly. "And possibly eat."

"Possibly?" Jessie turned on the porch with an inscrutable grin on her face. She crossed her arms and studied him for several moments before she spoke. "Do you have plans for lunch?"

"You doing okay?" He frowned at the unexpected invitation. Was she worried about staying alone at the ranch after her break-in? "Need me to stay?"

She came down two steps to meet him at eye level. "Are *you* doing okay? When was the last time you ate or slept?"

"I grabbed a Danish when I got our coffee."

Garrett wasn't exactly sure what career she had before investing her time and money into K-9 Ranch, but he suspected it was something like corporate raider or drill sergeant, based on the stern look she gave him. "When was the last time you ate anything that had vitamins and nutrients in it?"

"I'm not one of your dogs. You don't have to feed me or pat me on the head. I'm a grown man and can take care of myself."

"Well, you're doing a piss-poor job of it this morning from the look of things. You haven't shaved." She reached out and brushed a fingertip across his jaw, and he nearly flinched as every nerve impulse in his body seemed to wake up and rush to that single point of contact. "Not that the scruffy look doesn't work on you. But I know you take pride in looking professional. You're surviving on caffeine and sugar. And the lines beside your eyes are etched more deeply when you're tired like this. I've got plenty of leftovers I can heat up, or I can fix you soup and a sandwich."

Ignoring his body's disappointment at how abrupt

her touch had been, he eyed her skeptically. He was at-tracted to her, yes, but he cared about her well-being even more. "Does this have anything to do with what happened earlier this morning?"

"You mean my little freak-out?"

He liked that she didn't play dumb by pretending he was talking about anything other than that panic at-tack she'd had. "Are you trying to show me that noth-ing's wrong? That you're strong enough to take care of everyone else, from Mollie to Miss Eloise to me?" He zeroed in on those dove gray eyes. "When you should be taking care of yourself?"

Her chin came up, even as she hugged her arms around herself again. Yep, this woman wore invisible armor the same way he strapped on his flak vest every morning. "I'll admit that staying busy provides a dis-traction for me. But to quote a certain deputy—I'm *your* friend, too. 24/7. Feeding you lunch on a busy day is something friends do for each other. Besides, if you don't take care of yourself, you won't be any good to anybody. And we need you."

"We?"

"Jackson County. Your officers and staff. The Rus-sells. Miss Eloise." Her arms shifted and tightened. "Me."

Hearing her admit that she needed him, even so re-luctantly, sparked a tiny candle of hope inside him. Some of the fatigue in him eased at the idea of spend-ing time doing something that didn't require his badge and his gun for a while. And there was a definite appeal to spending that time with Jessie. "All right. A friendly lunch sounds nice. Talking about something other than work for thirty or forty minutes sounds even nicer." A breeze picked up a wavy tendril of hair that had fallen over her cheek, and he fought the urge to catch it between his fingers and smooth it back behind her ear. When she smiled at his response, she lit up like sunshine and vibrated with an energy that touched something hard and remote inside him and reminded certain parts of his anatomy that he was far from being over the hill. "Let me call in to my staff that I'm off the clock for thirty minutes or so, then I'll come inside and wash up."

"Let yourself in when you're ready. I'll be in the kitchen getting things heated up."

Heated up? Yep. The parts were definitely working. She was talking food, and his hormones kicked in as if she was coming on to him.

Before he could embarrass himself, or her, with the interest stirring behind his zipper, Garrett tapped the radio strapped to his shoulder and called in a Code 7, indicating he was taking a break from service to eat. He got a quick status report from his office manager, made note of a couple of items to follow up on and more tasks that he could delegate to officers on staff. Talking business generally dampened any sex drive and put him in the right frame of mind to share lunch with Jessie without spooking her.

"Jessie?" Shadow greeted him at the door when he stepped inside, seeming much happier to see him now than when he'd been holding Eloise's shotgun.

"Back here. Lock the door behind you, please."

"Will do." Garrett removed his hat and hung it on

a peg on the hall tree beside the stairs that led to the rooms on the second floor. Respecting her need for security, he turned the dead bolt in the front door before following Shadow through the front hallway that ran all the way back to the kitchen. He hung back in the archway of her homey gray and white kitchen, which was filled with both antiques and modern stainless steel appliances. He watched her set out bowls and pull a foil-wrapped loaf of something out of the oven. The enticing smells of whatever she was heating in the microwave made his stomach grumble again.

Jessie laughed and nodded toward the refrigerator. "There's sun tea in there. Or you can pour yourself a glass of milk or grab a bottle of water."

"May I get you a drink?"

"Tea, please. Hey, would you refill Shadow's water bowl? Last night, he left my room for a late-night snack, and I guess he knocked his feeding stand over in the dark." She smiled over at the long-haired shepherd mix who was walking in circles to find just the right spot to lie down on what Garrett suspected was one of several beds around the house. "Just toss that wet towel in the laundry room. Then sit and relax."

Jessie sliced corn bread and ladled up bowls of stew while Garrett completed his assignments. He felt himself relaxing at the normalcy of working together to complete domestic tasks. He'd been gone a lot in the early days of his marriage with training and deployments, while Hayley had run the house and taught kindergarten. But once he'd chaptered out of the Army to be with Haley those last two years, one of his favorite things was simply spending time with her—doing small jobs like these around the house while she supervised. Or sharing the work when she was strong enough to help. This felt a little like that, only different because Jessie was less fragile, and certainly more bossy than Haley had been. This felt almost date-like because they were spending some quality time together that had nothing to do with work. She trusted him enough to invite him into her space, to let him get acquainted with her routine. This time meant everything to him because he knew better than to take any moment for granted when it came to being with someone he cared about.

He reached for the faucet on the sink and his shoulder accidentally brushed against hers. When Jessie scuttled away from the unexpected contact, Garrett frowned and purposely moved some space between them.

That subtle revelation of discomfort beneath Jessie's welcoming facade erased his pensive smile and reminded him that this was neither a date nor domestic bliss, and that she seemed almost desperate to keep him at arm's length even though she was the one who'd invited him here. He circled around the kitchen island instead of taking the shorter route to Shadow's bed and feeding stand and set the water bowl on its rack.

He waited while she carried their plates to the antique oak farm table, keeping the width of one of the ladder back chairs between them. "Maybe while we're eating, you could explain a little bit about your flashback this morning."

She swung her gaze up to his. "Garrett—"

"I don't want to be the thing that triggers you. Whether it's the gun or my size or my gender, I want to know so I can avoid making things worse for you."

She reached across the chair to touch his forearm, her fingers sliding against the eagle inked there. So, she wasn't averse to touching him. But she wanted to control how it happened. Her skin warmed his, and his nerve endings woke with eager possibilities again. Still holding his gaze with a wry smile, she pressed her fingertips into the muscle there. "You don't make things worse for me. And I'd never want you to stop being the man you are." With one final squeeze, she released him and pulled out the chair opposite his. "To be honest, I'm not sure what set me off this morning. Probably a combination of things. Or something subconscious that I'm not aware of. If you don't mind, I wouldn't mind talking it through with someone."

"I don't mind." He pushed in her chair for her before taking his seat.

A few minutes later, he was digging into a bowl of fragrant, hearty beef stew and a slice of corn bread slathered in butter and honey. He let her eat a healthy portion of her meal before he pushed her to share some of her story with him. "I know you've been a victim of violence. You told me your husband was shot and killed."

"Wow. When I said I wanted to talk, you jumped right to the heart of the matter."

"We can talk about the weather or the prospects for Royals baseball this year, if you prefer."

"No." Jessie set her spoon on her plate and pushed the rest of her lunch away. "John was killed by the ex-husband of one of his clients. Lee Palmer didn't like the divorce settlement John negotiated. I think he blamed John for the whole divorce going through. When John saw what was happening, he pushed me away, right before Palmer shot him in the head."

Garrett made a mental note to look up Lee Palmer and make sure the man was sitting on death row for murdering an officer of the court. He kept his voice gentle, trying not to sound like a county deputy push-ing for answers. "Did something about Miss Eloise or this rash of petty crimes trigger a flashback?"

"I don't think so. I mean, I wasn't thrilled that she was pointing a gun at us." Her gaze drifted over to the bed where Shadow was snoring. "Palmer killed our dog that day, too."

Garrett polished off the last of his corn bread, wait-ing for her to continue.

"Zeus, our dog at the time, went after that guy with a vengeance after Palmer shot John. He attacked him and held him at bay long enough so I could get away." He hated the clinical way she was reciting the facts, and suspected that was yet another way she coped with the trauma of that day. "I locked myself in the bathroom, called 9-1-1—although neighbors had also reported the shooting and the police were already on their way. That bastard shot him. Zeus gave his life so that I could live."

"That explains your need to rescue all of these dogs. They're like your children. You raise them well. You train them to do what your Zeus did if necessary. Make sure they all have good homes and a purpose. It's a noble way to honor his sacrifice." He leaned back against his chair, keeping the hand that had curled into a fist at her story hidden beneath the table. "Eloise pointed a gun at your dogs."

"I didn't panic when Eloise had the gun."

"You panicked when *I* had it. Shadow growled at me. *I* was a bigger threat."

She shook her head. Then she pushed to her feet and carried their plates and bowls to the sink, obviously needing a break from the heavy topic. "You always carry a gun. I'm not sure that's it, either."

As much as he wanted to believe she wasn't afraid of him, even subconsciously, he had to make sure. "What did the shooter look like?"

"Nothing like you. Shorter. Younger. Beer belly. Desperately needed a shower." He could see her dredge up the memory. She grasped the edge of the sink and squeezed her eyes shut against it. "Wild brown eyes."

Garrett beat back the urge to go to her, to take her in his arms and offer comfort. But she'd asked for a sounding board, someone to talk to, someone to help her figure this out. He was the guy who solved mysteries. That's who she needed right now. And he'd be damned if he'd be anything else but exactly what she needed.

"He was a man." Garrett suggested another possibility. "Any man threatening you could be a trigger."

"No." She came back and sat in the chair right beside him. "The guns don't help. The dogs protecting me could be part of it. But I think…my emotions…"

Her eyes lost their focus. "In my head, I was losing everything that mattered all over again."

"What mattered? You lost your husband to violence. Zeus."

She pulled her hands from the tabletop and splayed her fingers over her stomach, as if she was caressing something precious. "I was eight months pregnant when I was shot. I lost the baby, our little boy. He was my last link to John, and… The damage was too severe. The surgeon removed my uterus, tubes, and ovaries. I lost the ability to ever have children."

He bit back his curse at the injustice of this woman being denied the child she clearly had wanted. "I don't remind you of a baby, do I?"

Her gaze snapped up to his. "Of course not."

"Do I look like your husband?" He wasn't doing a very good job of keeping the edge out of his tone. He understood violence and loss. He'd taken lives and buried loved ones. The injustice of all Jessie had suffered ate away his ability to be the impartial sounding board she'd asked for.

"John had dark hair, too. But he had more of a runner's build. Wore a suit and tie to work. You're…beefy. More…" She shook her head. "Not really."

"What was different this morning?" he pressed. "What mattered that you thought you were going to lose?"

Jessie considered his question, studied him intently. He thought he saw a glimmer of understanding darken her eyes. Then shock quickly took its place. Oh, hell. The resolve that was guarded and cautious and willing to wait for this woman crumbled into dust as he processed all she wasn't saying.

Eloise had pointed the gun at *him*, too.

"Me? Did you think you were going to lose *me*?"

She never answered because Shadow's feeding stand slammed into the end of the cabinet. "What the…?" A muffled whimpering noise and clear thumping against the cabinet pushed Jessie to her feet. Garrett followed her to the dog's bed near the back door to discover Shadow lying on his side with his legs stretched out and twitching as if he was trying to swim. "Is he having a dream? Shadow!" Jessie dropped to her knees, her hands hovering above her beloved pet as if she wasn't sure how or if she should touch him. "What's wrong?"

Garrett knelt beside her and took in the dog's drooling and small, but rapid, head movements. "Looks like he's having a seizure." Jessie placed her hand gently on the dog's flank. The fact that he didn't startle and wake to her touch confirmed his suspicion. "Has he seized before?"

"No. Is this what happened last night? I don't understand."

He'd had enough training as a medic to start asking questions. "Who's your vet?"

"Hazel Cooper-Burke."

"In KC?"

Jessie nodded without looking up. She was trying to pet the dog, but he kept jerking beneath her hands. "He's hot to the touch. I don't know what to do."

Garrett clasped her by the shoulders and pulled her to her feet. "Call Dr. Coop." Now that she'd been given a task, she nodded and pulled her phone from her jeans. Meanwhile, Garrett scooped up the shaking dog and carried him out to his truck, bed and all. Jessie grabbed her purse and followed right on his heels. "Jedediah Burke's wife?" he clarified. "I know Sergeant Burke through the KCPD K-9 unit." He nodded toward the crew cab's back door handle and Jessie pulled it open. He gently laid the large dog on the seat and scooted him over to make room for a passenger. "Get in the back. She's in a new building after that bomb took out the old one. I know where I'm going."

"I will. Thanks, Hazel. We're on our way." Jessie ended the call and juggled the items in her hands to put them away. "She says to bring him right in. It could last anywhere from thirty seconds to five minutes. It's been more than thirty seconds, hasn't it? I'm supposed to time it. She asked if he had a head injury? If he'd been hit by a car? Has he eaten anything he shouldn't? Caffeine? Chocolate? He's been with me all morning. I don't know what—"

Garrett tagged her behind the neck to stop her panicking and help her focus. His palm fit perfectly against the nape of her neck. He tunneled his fingers beneath the base of her ponytail and loosened some of the silky waves of hair, willing her to catch her breath. "Get in the back and buckle up. Comfort him. I'll get you there as fast as I can."

Jessie's gaze locked on to his. She wound her fingers around his wrist and squeezed her understanding. "Thank you for being here with me."

He leaned in and pressed a kiss to her forehead. "Nowhere else I'd rather be. Get in."

Once he closed the door behind her, Garrett climbed in behind the wheel, turned on the lights and siren, and raced toward the highway.

Chapter Four

"Idiopathic epilepsy?" Jessica stroked her fingers through Shadow's fur while Dr. Hazel Cooper-Burke finished a routine examination on the dog on the metal exam table between them. "What's that?"

Shadow lay there like the Sphinx, his head up, his tongue out and gently panting, his demeanor as relaxed as any other visit to the vet's office these past ten years. Other than a few pokes of a needle, he liked the staff here and knew there would be a treat for him at the end of the visit. His present behavior seemed so normal that Jessica found it heartbreaking to think how out of it he'd been at the house almost an hour earlier. Despite Garrett leaning against the wall behind her and Hazel being a good friend, she was reluctant to break contact with the dog who meant so much to her.

Dr. Cooper-Burke finished her exam and ruffled the fur around Shadow's ears and muzzle. "Good boy." Shadow ate up the attention before demolishing the treat Hazel rewarded him with. "Basically, it means we don't know what's causing it. With Shadow's age, we know it's not genetic epilepsy—he would have shown the symptoms long before now. I see no signs of a head injury or heat stroke. It could be a brain tumor. Something in his diet. It could be aging and cognitive decline."

Jessica frowned, frustrated that the vet couldn't give her a definitive answer. "Shadow's as smart and alert as he ever was. And nothing has changed in his diet, although, it's possible he could have gotten into something he shouldn't."

Garrett pushed away from the wall and came to stand beside her. "You think someone poisoned him?"

Jessica glanced up, sharing her explanation with both friends. "Not everyone is a fan of my dogs. Even though it's private property, I'm certified, and it's a completely licensed and vetted business."

"I'm guessing if it was intentional poisoning, he'd have vomiting or diarrhea. And he seems perfectly fine now. Plus, you might have other dogs showing symptoms." Hazel reached across Shadow's back to squeeze her hand. "Jessica, it could be as simple and heartbreaking as an end-of-life thing. A dog his size and age…"

"Shadow's dying?" The question came out almost a sob, although she already felt cried out after the fast drive into the city to the vet clinic. She immediately felt Garrett's hand at her back, its warmth seeping into her skin and short-circuiting the impulse to break down again. "There's nothing you can do?"

Hazel hastened to reassure her. "Eleven years old for a dog his size is pretty advanced. And I'm guessing life wasn't kind to him before you took him in. Look at all the gray in his muzzle. Sadly, it's the natural progression of things."

"I know." Understanding the situation logically didn't feel like much of a balm to her psyche. She pressed against Garrett's hand, reining in any pending sense of loss and kept it together so that she could understand all the necessary facts. "What does this mean for Shadow? What should I expect?"

"I can treat the symptoms. Idiopathic epilepsy isn't going to kill him, and he doesn't feel any pain while he's seizing. But it's a neurological disorder that can come with aging. It's all about his quality of life now. As long as he'll take the diazepam pill with a bite of cheese or a dog treat when he starts to seize, we'll go that route. If swallowing becomes an issue, the seizures become frequent or last longer than a few minutes, we'll switch to a larger dose through a suppository." She turned away to get the prescription bottle her vet tech had set on the counter and handed it to Jessica. "You're okay giving him the pill?"

"Of course. I have other dogs who get medications."

Hazel smiled. "I never worry about a Jess Bennington dog because I know you'll take good care of him. Let's follow up to see how things are going in another month, okay? He may not have a seizure between now and then, but if he does, give him the pill and be sure to time the length of it, then give me a call."

"I will."

"Any questions?"

Jessica leaned over to kiss the top of Shadow's head. "If this is an end-of-life thing, how long does Shadow have?"

"He's in good health, otherwise. Possibly a year. Maybe a little more or less."

Jessica wasn't quite ready to process what that meant. Shadow had brought her out of the depths of her grief and anger. He'd given her someone to love, something to trust without fail. He'd inspired the idea of K-9 Ranch, given this new version of her life a purpose. She couldn't picture what life without him would look like. But he'd given her so much over the years, she also knew she'd do whatever was necessary to make his remaining time as rich and comfortable as possible.

"Thanks, Hazel." She tucked the prescription into her shoulder bag and helped Shadow down. Then she circled around the table to hug her friend, silently thanking her for her care and kindness to both her and her patient. When she pulled away, she glanced up at Garrett. "I'm ready to go whenever you are."

He settled his hand on the small of her back again and guided her out the door. He paused to shake hands with the vet. "Thanks, Dr. Coop. Say hi to Burke for me."

"I will."

He held on to the veterinarian's hand and glanced toward the front entrance. "It's getting dark outside. Is Burke coming to pick you up? Or do you want me to wait and walk you out?"

Hazel shook the bangs of her short pixie cut hair. "Careful, Jessica. I think this one is as overprotective as my Burke is. When you've had a day as tough as this one has been, let him do his thing and take care of you. You can be strong again tomorrow."

It was on the tip of Jessica's tongue to correct her friend's perception of her relationship with Garrett. But Hazel's advice sounded pretty good right now. And she couldn't deny how much worse this life-changing news would have been without Garrett at her side. "He has been awfully good to me today."

"I suspected as much." Hazel traded one more hug before pulling away and looking up at Garrett. "Take care of my friend, okay? This is going to be tough for her."

"I'll do my best."

She scooted them toward the front door. "I'll lock up behind you. I'll be fine. Burke and Gunny both should be here in a few minutes."

At the mention of Hazel's husband and his K-9 partner, Garrett nodded and led Jessica out to the parking lot.

She was exhausted from the tension that had been vibrating through her from the moment she realized something was wrong with Shadow. Since the dog was feeling fine now, he wanted to sit up in the back seat and stick his nose out the window of Garrett's truck. She settled into the front passenger seat, tipped her head back against the headrest, and closed her eyes. The moment he climbed in and started the engine, she rolled her head toward him and studied his rugged profile and indomitable strength. That strength had gotten her through today, just as Hazel had said, and she was grateful. "What am I going to do without Shadow? He's my…everything. I can't lose him."

He turned those handsome green eyes to her. "You're

not going to find out today. Let me get you two home. We'll drive through someplace and get dinner so you don't have to cook."

When he pulled out of the parking lot, she turned her head back to look out the window. The streetlights were coming on and rush hour traffic was beginning to thin out as they drove out of the city. Hazel had stayed late after closing for her. Too many people had done too much for her today. She needed to be more self-sufficient than this. "I'm not hungry."

"Taking care of a friend goes both ways, Jessie. You have to eat something. You need to keep your strength up so you can take care of Shadow. He'll worry about you if you don't."

The dog would worry? *Smooth, Caldwell.* She almost smiled, but that required more energy than she had at the moment. And what she *should* do wasn't the same as what she wanted. So, she took Hazel's advice to heart. "Will you stay with me for a while? I mean, eat dinner with me?"

"I have to go inside your place, anyway. Left my hat there. Clever of me, wasn't it? Made sure I had a reason to come by and see you again, whether you invited me or not?"

She knew there was a teasing response to that goofy reasoning, but she didn't seem able to do lighthearted right now. "Never mind. You've already done so much for me today, and that's after pulling an all-nighter. You need to sleep."

Garrett grumbled something in his throat, and the glimpse of humor he'd tried to cajole her with disappeared. "I'm coming to your house for dinner, Jessie. And I'm staying as long as you need me."

"As my friend." She needed to remind herself of the distinction. That she was strong and whole—well, whole enough—and didn't need a man to take care of her. But it had been a blessing to have this one around today.

"As whatever you need."

GARRETT WRAPPED UP the cheeseburger Jessie had barely touched and stuck it in the fridge in case she was hungry later. If nothing else, she could give the meat to Shadow. He had a feeling that dog was going to be spoiled rotten now that she knew he was nearing the end of his life.

He gathered up the rest of the trash from the burger joint where they'd stopped and put it in the trash can under the sink while Jessie loaded their plates into the dishwasher. At least, she'd polished off her fries and a couple of his, along with most of a chocolate milkshake. It wasn't the healthiest of meals, but it was better than trying to go to sleep with a stomach that was empty and a head that was full of worry.

Jessie had a little more color in her face than she'd had earlier. But her movements seemed strained and sluggish, as if she was sleepwalking and simply going through the motions of cleaning up after a late dinner. Not for the first time that night, she wandered over to the edge of the counter to glance down at Shadow lying in his bed. The dog appeared to be as tired as his mistress, but he still raised his head and looked up at her. "It's all right, boy." She reached down to scratch around his ears. "I haven't forgotten. We'll go in a few minutes."

"Go? Go where?" he asked.

"Nightly rounds around the kennels. Make sure the dogs are all okay before we turn in." She propped her elbows on the counter and rested her chin in her hand, still watching Shadow as he settled back down in his bed. "Everything about him feels so normal, like he's the same old Shadow I've always known."

Garrett moved to the edge of the counter beside her and rested his elbows on the granite top. "You need him, don't you."

She nodded, and once more Garrett was struck by the urge to touch the long tendril of silvery-gold hair that hung against her cheek and brush it gently behind her ear. "He's more than a pet. More than a protector. He was my sanity when I couldn't move past losing John and the baby. My security blanket. He rescued me more than I ever rescued him."

No, what he really wanted to do was release her hair from its ponytail and comb his fingers through its long, wavy length—find out if it was as silky and voluminous as it looked once it was freed from its restraints. But he schooled his hormonal impulses and settled for butting his shoulder gently against hers. "He's a lucky dog."

She nudged his shoulder right back. "I'm a lucky mama."

He considered what she'd told him earlier about all she had lost—not just her husband and pet, but the chance to be a mother. No wonder she was gun-shy about starting a new relationship. He and Hayley had never had kids. First, he'd been gone, and then, no matter how hard they tried, they hadn't been able to get the timing right. Then she'd been sick, and there'd been no time at all. Not having kids was one of his biggest regrets. As a soldier and officer of the law, he might not be the best bet because of the inherent dangers of his job. But Hayley would have made a great mother. She was so patient and energetic with her students, and she'd taught them so much.

He glanced down at Jessie. She'd have made a wonderful mother, too. She'd be a strong role model for any daughter, a caring example for any son, and a staunch supporter for any cause or activity they might be interested in. He supposed that was why Shadow being diagnosed with idiopathic epilepsy was such a blow to her. Her dogs were her children. She raised them, took care of them, trained them, loved them. Then she sent her dogs out into the world to help others. Today she probably felt a lot like she was losing her child all over again.

Garrett reached over and pulled Jessie's hand from her chin. He splayed his larger hand against hers, then laced their fingers together—drawing her attention up to him and forging a tender connection. "I know you're exhausted. Why don't you head on up to bed, and I'll check the kennels for you before I go."

"*You're* the one who must be exhausted. The dogs are my responsibility. Besides, it will give Shadow one more time outside to do his business tonight."

He wasn't surprised that she was trying to reset the

boundaries between them. But she shouldn't be surprised that he was going to fight to maintain the new closeness that had sprung up between them today. "Then let me grab my jacket from my truck and I'll come with you."

"Garrett—"

"Humor me." When she straightened up and tried to pull away, he tightened his grip and cradled her hand between both of his. "You had a shotgun pointed at you this morning. You had a PTSD episode. You shared some disturbing details about your husband's murder and got bad news about Shadow. Dr. Coop was right. I feel a little overprotective where you're concerned. I'm not going to apologize for wanting to make sure nothing else happens to you."

She did surprise him by reaching up and laying her free hand against his stubbled jaw. Such a sweet, gentle touch. And his body was crazy to absorb as many of those casual caresses as she wanted to give out. "Thank you. I'd appreciate the company. I don't particularly want to run into one of your vandals by myself out there."

Nodding at her agreement, he pulled away and went out to his truck to pull on his uniform jacket. The calendar might say it was spring, but the night air was cool and overcast. The long-range forecast called for rain and warmer temperatures that would green things up. But until the warm front came through, it felt more like autumn than spring.

Although Jessie had some outdoor lighting at the kennels and barn, he grabbed the flashlight from his glove compartment and met her and Shadow around the side of the house. At the reminder of the mini crime spree, he felt better safe than sorry about making sure they had a secure path. The dog trotted on ahead, following where his nose was taking him, yet often looking back to make sure Jessie was still in sight as they walked the length of the outbuilding that housed her rescue dogs. Garrett refilled some water bowls with a hose while she greeted each dog by name and petted them through the fencing as well as checking to make sure each latch was secure.

"You keep them all locked up at night?" he asked, rolling up the long water hose and hanging it at the end of the building.

"Except for Rex and Toby. They're trained to guard the property, and I don't worry about them running off. Although Rex likes to bunk down with the goats in the barn, instead of using his doghouse." Just then, Toby trotted out of his own doghouse and jogged up to them, his whole butt wagging with excitement at the late-night visit. "And Mr. Personality here bunks wherever it suits him. Sometimes, his doghouse. Sometimes, the front porch. Sometimes, in the barn with his big buddy. Who's my good Toby?" She petted the black Lab around his face and ears. Then, when Garrett patted his chest, the energetic dog rose up on his hind legs and braced his front paws against him so that Garrett had full access to rubbing his flanks and tummy. "I think he likes you."

"We had a hunting dog like Toby growing up. Ace was more subdued, though." He pushed the dog down and Toby trotted back to his doghouse, where he picked up a rawhide chew and lay down to enjoy his treat.

"Where'd you get that, boy?" Jessie asked, frowning. "Did you find that treat in the barn?" She turned her attention to the well-maintained red structure. "There was a shattered treat jar in the storage room. I wonder if he got in there once the door was busted open. Or if whoever broke in tossed him a treat to distract him."

Garrett heard the suspicion in her tone, but he had already turned his light toward a sign he found even more worrisome. "How many clients do you usually have out here during the day?"

"Two or three. Unless I'm having a group training session. Then it can be up to ten or twelve." She walked up behind where he had knelt to study the curving driveway and parking area. "Why?"

Shadow came up beside him and dipped his nose to the tire track Garrett was inspecting. "What do you think, buddy? Does this look off to you?"

Shadow sat back on his haunches and raised his dark eyes to him. Garrett interpreted that as a tacit agreement to his suspicions.

"Garrett?"

He stood and pointed out what he was seeing with his flashlight. Several rows of tire tracks were imbedded in the dirt and gravel leading from the main drive to the barn. The tracks crisscrossed each other to the extent it would be hard to determine the exact course of the vehicles that had left them. But he counted at least five different tread marks, including a distinctive asymmetrical tread usually used by souped-up sports cars or off-roaders. Not something the meek Mollie Crane on a budget or an old farm truck would use. He pulled out his phone and snapped pictures of each distinctive tread. "You had company out here while we were in KC."

Jessie crossed her arms beside him. "I forgot to text Soren and let him know I was gone. He probably stopped by for his shift to feed the dogs. They're all in their kennels, and the goats are in their stall, so someone took care of them. I'll text him in the morning to confirm."

He visually followed the dusty tracks. "If this was Soren, he didn't come alone. These extra tracks weren't here when we went inside for lunch."

"I canceled my afternoon appointments before we left Hazel's office. Do you think whoever broke into the storage room came back for something else?" He could see her visibly shivering in the cool air. "Sometimes, people get lost and turn around in the driveway." She shook her head, dismissing the possible explanation, even as she said it. "But not this many vehicles in one day. And there's room to turn around by the house. They wouldn't come this far onto the property unless they were coming to see me. Or my dogs." She turned back to the kennels, "Do you think the dogs are okay?"

Garrett caught her by the elbow before she could charge back to the kennels. "You've already checked every last one of your charges for yourself. They're fine. Here. I don't know if you're spooked or you're cold. But this will help." He shrugged out of his sheriff's department jacket and wrapped it around her shoulders. "Better?"

"Probably a little of both," she admitted, offering him a weary smile as she shoved her arms into the sleeves and overlapped the front beneath her chin. "You are a furnace, my friend. Thank you."

"You're welcome." Once he was certain she wasn't on the verge of panic over her dogs again, he shined his flashlight up at the device anchored above the barn door. "Is that a security camera?"

She nodded. "I've got one that points down toward the kennels and the training yard, and one at the front gate so I can tell when company is coming."

Cameras were a good thing. Cameras might finally give him the answers he needed. "Do they record? Or are they real-time monitors?"

"They back up the live feed for twenty-four hours at a time on my computer unless I make a copy." She burrowed her fingers into Shadow's fur beside her. "I can go up to the house and pull up the feed. See if I recognize any of the vehicles."

"Mind if I come with you?" The dust had settled in these tracks, indicating whoever had made them was long gone. He could conduct a more thorough search of the grounds, but his gut was telling him he wouldn't find anything.

"Of course, not." She fell into step beside him as they headed back to the house. "You don't need to check the perimeter or follow those tracks to see where they lead?"

"No. Whatever happened out here is over and done.

I'll get one of my officers to drive out and look around. Let's get you in the house."

The hairs at the nape of his neck were sticking straight out with a subconscious alert that something was very, very wrong here. He was still waiting for the big event he suspected all these little criminal hiccups were leading up to. His years as a sniper, learning the patience to lie in wait until his target appeared—and all his years of experience with the sheriff's department—kept telling him that something was about to hit the fan big-time. And the fact that several of them were centered around Jessie didn't sit well with him. He needed to stay sharp and figure out what was going on before Jessie or anyone else got hurt.

Several minutes later, they were sipping on fresh cups of decaf coffee—Jessie's doctored up with cream and sugar—and sitting in front of the computer in her office. They'd fast-forwarded through the daylight hours, getting glimpses of Mollie Crane's small car and Hugo's truck, and Garrett's heavy-duty departmental pickup. The images had gotten darker as night set in, and slightly distorted by the light above the camera.

"There's Soren." She stopped the scrolling images and pointed to the screen. The teenager was climbing out of the passenger side of a car. "I recognize his ponytail. Toby runs up to meet him. He recognizes him, so no one sounds an alarm. But that's not Soren's car."

Garrett braced his elbows on his knees and leaned forward to study the grainy image. "Can you print me a copy of that?"

"Sure."

The printer whirred in the background while Garrett squinted at the screen. "Do you recognize the driver?"

"No. Soren's late, too. He's supposed to come at five o'clock, but the sun would still be up then." She still huddled inside his jacket, apparently unable to shake the chill from outside. She took another sip of her hot drink and cradled it between her fingers. It would be so easy to drape his arm around her shoulders and share some of his body heat, or even pick her up and set her on his lap in the same chair and wrap her up against his thighs and chest. More body heat meant a warmer Jessie.

More body heat meant trouble.

"Ready to see more?" Jessie's question startled him from the decadent spiral of his thoughts.

Man, he was tired. He shoved his fingers through his hair. He couldn't even drum up the willpower to keep his lusty thoughts about Jessie buried inside where they couldn't distract him with false hope. "Yeah. I'll run that picture by Hugo, see if he recognizes his grand-son's friend."

"Garrett?" He flinched as her warm hand settled on his knee. "Are you okay? We can do this tomorrow. You need your rest."

Garrett covered her hand with his before she could pull it away. Damn those gentle touches of hers. They stirred up his senses and sneaked beneath his skin, giving him a glimpse of how good a relationship between them could be. If only she felt the same connection he did. Correction, if only she'd allow herself to feel the connection they shared.

"There has to be more on this recording. I want to finish it up."

"And find answers to your mystery?"

He squeezed her hand beneath his. "Yeah. It's hard to relax when there are loose ends bugging me like this."

He was more pleased than he should have been when she left her hand clasped in his and set down her coffee to continue scrolling through the recording.

"Stop." Garrett was the one who finally broke the connection when a dark Dodge Charger drove onto the screen. "Who's that?"

"Look at the bling on that," she pointed out unnecessarily. "No teenager can afford that car." Without asking, she was already printing out a picture of the sports car. "I have no idea who that is. Can you make out the license plate?"

He pinched the bridge of his nose and rubbed his eyes. They burned with fatigue, but if he blinked enough, they would clear, and he could study the images more closely.

"A partial. He left the souped-up tire tracks." The glare from the headlights obscured the vehicle identification and passengers inside, and when they made a U-turn and sped away, they kicked up enough dust and gravel to see only a glimpse of the generic Missouri license plate. "Hopefully, it's enough to run." He pulled out his phone and called the sheriff's station. "Caldwell here. I need you to run a partial plate for me on a Dodge Charger. Black or dark blue. Over-the-top trim and underglow lights." The officer covering the night shift took down the info. "I know it's not much. Find out what you can and get back to me. I want a

BOLO out on the car. If it shows up anywhere between Kansas City and Lone Jack, I want to know about it."

"Yes, sir."

Jessie slowly scrolled the images forward while Garrett ended the call, then rewound them to the beginning of the clip. "What do they want?"

"Nothing good." Any clear view of the driver was obscured by the headlights, although he was of slighter stature than the guy who got out on the passenger side. The baggy jeans and loose jacket made Garrett think the guy was carrying a weapon. And there was no way to get a description of his face. Even with darkness falling, he wore dark glasses and a cap pulled low over his forehead. "Can you make out any identifying marks on his hat or jacket?"

She shook her head. "A sports logo, maybe. The picture on his hat could be barbells? It's not like when Soren and his friend stopped by. This guy gets out of his car, and Toby and the other dogs raise a ruckus. The moment Rex runs out of the barn to check out who's there, both men get back in and drive away."

He reached down to scratch Shadow around his ears. The dog had settled below the desk at Jessie's feet. "Thank God for your dogs. Or we probably would have had another incident."

"You think these are the same guys who broke into the Russells' cabin and terrorized Miss Eloise's chickens?"

"These guys don't look like vandals to me. And they're clearly not good ol' country boys. There's too much money in their clothes and car."

"Illegal money?"

He couldn't prove it just by studying a grainy image, but his years of experience told him the answer was yes. "Probably drugs or moving stolen goods. Or something to do with your dogs."

"Like dog fighting? I have one pit bull rescue out there, but she's not even a year old." He watched the color drain from her cheeks. "Do you think they were here to steal bait dogs?"

"We don't know anything yet." He squeezed her knee as he pushed himself upright and stretched the kinks in his back and shoulders. "Let's not go there."

She glanced over and caught him yawning behind his hand. "I'll zoom in as much as I can and print a picture for you."

"Would you copy the whole thing to a flash drive for me? I'd like to go over it again tomorrow when my eyes are fresh." He smirked. No sense hiding the truth. "Better yet, I'll have one of my officers whose eyes are twenty years younger than mine take a look at it."

"Garrett, you need to go to bed."

"Pot calling the kettle black, Ms. Bennington. You've been on a long, emotional roller-coaster ride today." He checked his watch. "Good grief. It's two in the morning."

"I don't think I'll be sleeping much tonight." She mimicked his yawn while she waited for the image to print and dug a flash drive out of her desk. "Shadow seems so normal now. Like that seizure never even happened." She inserted the data stick to copy the video file. "But now I know there's this time bomb inside his head, and it could go off at any time."

Garrett pushed to his feet and returned his chair to the kitchen table. "Dr. Cooper-Burke said it could be weeks or months before he seizes again."

"Or it could be days." Her soft gray eyes were watery with unshed tears as she followed him to the kitchen and handed over the evidence he'd requested. He was surprised at how right it felt for her to walk past his outstretched hand and line her body up against his. She curled her fingers into the front of his wrinkled uniform shirt and rested her forehead at the juncture of his neck and shoulder. "I can't lose him, Garrett."

"Honey, you're exhausted." He dropped the photos and flash drive on the table behind her and wrapped his arms around her. He wished he'd taken off his flak vest so he could feel her curves and heat pressed against him. But he wasn't about to push her away to do so. "Why don't you take him upstairs and get ready for bed. You can watch over him until you fall asleep."

She felt the barrier of protective armor between them, too, because she lightly rapped against his vest. "This isn't very conducive to cuddling, Deputy," she teased.

Garrett tightened his arms more securely around her. "Don't worry. I can still keep you warm."

"And keep the demons away?"

He pressed a kiss to her forehead. "I'll try."

Her fingers found the edge of his vest and curled beneath it. "What if Shadow has a seizure in the middle of the night? What if I'm asleep and can't help him?"

"This is going to be your new normal for a while. You'll figure it all out." When she steadied her emotions with a deep breath, he made an offer. "Would you feel better if I stayed? Kept an eye on things while you sleep?"

Strands of her silky hair caught in his beard stubble as she shook her head. "You can't stay awake two nights in a row."

"I'm not going to leave if you need me. I'm a light sleeper. If I hear something, I'll wake up." She pulled back, considering his suggestion for several seconds. When he saw the polite dismissal forming on her lips, he argued his case. "I know you've got guest rooms upstairs, or the couch is fine. I'll sleep better, too, if I'm here. That way I'll know you're safe, that you don't have any trespassers, and the horrible things I can imagine happening during the ten minutes it would take me to get to you won't keep me awake."

She reached up and threaded her fingers through the messy spikes of his hair and tried to smooth them into place. More gentle touches. This woman was so damn addictive. "Then the practical thing would be for you to stay with me tonight. That way, we can both get a good night's sleep."

"I can work with that." She pulled away entirely and wrapped his jacket more tightly around her, in lieu of his arms. He'd take that swap, knowing his jacket was going to retain some of that faint lilac scent that clung to her skin. Soap or lotion, he imagined. "Go on up and get ready for bed. I'm going to walk around the house and check things out one more time."

She motioned for Shadow to come to her side. "I'll set out a new toothbrush for you in the main bathroom upstairs. Need anything else?"

"I'm good."

"Good night, Garrett."

"Good night."

By the time he returned after securing the entire house, inside and out, and after one more call to the C shift to drive by Jessie's ranch a couple of times through the remainder of the night, he crept back upstairs to find her asleep on top of her bed, with Shadow stretched out beside her. Although she'd left a lamp on for him in the guest room across the hall, Garrett lingered a moment in her doorway, taking in the sweetly homey sight.

She'd conked out in her clothes, her hand resting on the dog's shoulder. She'd hung his jacket over the back of a chair where she'd tossed her insulated vest and kicked off her lace-up boots. But she still wore her long-sleeved T-shirt, socks, and jeans. She'd brushed her hair out in silver and gold waves that flared over the pillowcase behind her, and he felt his weary body stirring with the desire to bury his nose in those glorious waves and claim this brave, battered by life—but refusing to be beaten—woman for his own.

Needing to move away from that dream before he did anything to ruin the gentle tension that had been simmering between them all day, Garrett quickly brushed his teeth and took care of business. He stripped down to his T-shirt and pants before coming back to her doorway for one last reassurance that she was safe.

Jessie had rolled over, and in the dim light from across the hall he watched her eyes blink open into slits, then close again. "That's not sleeping," she murmured drowsily. "That's hovering in the doorway and staying awake." She stretched out her hand without raising it off the bed. "If the guest room is too far away for you to relax, stay with me."

The tension inside him settled at her invitation. "You're sure?"

"I have a feeling you won't sleep if you don't have eyes on me." She paused to cover her adorably big yawn. "This isn't a seduction, Garrett. Nothing's going to happen. There's a dog in bed with us."

"I'd like to hold you," he confessed.

"I'm okay with that." Her eyes opened fully to meet his gaze. "I'm having a hard time shaking the chill of the night outside. Or maybe it's all in my head. But I could use the body heat."

Body heat. Garrett bit back a groan. But out loud he said, "Happy to be of help."

He went back to the guest room to turn off the light and grab his gun and holster. When he returned, she'd dozed off again. He set his weapon within reach on the bedside table, then climbed in beside her.

But she wasn't as asleep as he thought. The moment his head hit the pillow, she scooted closer and snuggled into him, one arm folded between them, the other resting across his waist. She nestled her cheek against his shoulder and buried her nose at the base of his neck. He slipped his arm behind her back and held her loosely against his side. But she pulled her top leg over his thighs and slipped her toes down between his knees, wrapping herself around him as if she was using him for a body pillow. "An absolute furnace." She buried her lips and nose against his neck. "Mmm…you smell good."

"I smell like a forty-eight-hour shift and too much time in dusty barns, vet's offices, and at crime scenes."

"Mmm-hmm."

"Jessie?" This time, there was no answer. She was more asleep than awake now, and they were snuggled up as close as two people still wearing most of their clothes could get. Who knew this prickly, independent woman was such a cuddler? It was another glimpse of vulnerability he'd do his damnedest to protect. He indulged his senses by tangling his fingers through her silky hair and bringing it to his nose to breathe in her flowery scent. Then he pressed a kiss to her forehead. "Sleep, hon. I've got you." He reached across her to rest one hand on her precious Shadow. "I've got you both."

This was the closeness and contentment that was missing from his life. Sure, he wanted to find out what kind of passion was locked up behind Jessie's protective walls. He wanted to kiss her until she couldn't think of any man but him and feel her body come to life beneath his. But he wanted this, too. He needed this.

With the woman he was falling hard and fast for secure in his arms, Garrett finally surrendered to his body's bone-numbing fatigue and fell into a deep sleep.

Chapter Five

Garrett woke up feeling surprisingly refreshed, even after only a few hours of sleep. But the schedule that had been ingrained in him years ago by the military and law enforcement meant he was an early riser. Most mornings he did some kind of workout. On others, he drank his coffee and read his newspaper or reports that needed his attention.

This morning, he wanted nothing more than to linger in bed with the woman still tucked up against his side, breathing evenly in restful sleep. But an eager panting from across the bed made him suspect his morning had already been planned for him.

The moment he began to stir, Shadow raised his head from his spot on the other side of Jessie. The two males acknowledged each other. And, by mutual agreement, neither of them made a sound as Garrett extricated himself from the cheek resting on his chest and the arm curled around his waist. Shadow quietly jumped down while Garrett pulled his jacket from the chair and tucked it around Jessie since they'd slept on top of the covers. He put on his shoes, hit the john, and went downstairs with Shadow following closely on his heels.

Several minutes later, the dog was happily munching on his breakfast and Garrett was carrying two steaming mugs of coffee back up to Jessie's bedroom. He found her squinting against the sunlight that peeked around the curtains at the window. "You awake?"

Jessie stretched out the kinks in her limbs. But when she breathed in deeply, her eyes popped wide-open. "Is that coffee?"

Garrett chuckled at her hopeful response. "Yes. I thought I'd spoil you a little this morning. Helped myself, too."

"That's fine." She propped the pillows against the headboard and sat up, her cheeks pink with the anticipation flowing through her. Garrett set their mugs on the bedside table and perched on the edge of the bed facing her. Her soft smile was prettier than any sunrise. And her eyes, rested and no longer red with tears, reminded him of the moon on a cold, clear night.

When Garrett reached out to brush her hair off her cheek and tuck it behind her ear, she mimicked the caress. She combed her fingers through his hair in a hopeless attempt to tame the unruly spikes. Another smile. "It never cooperates, does it."

Her gentle touches nourished a hungry spot in his soul that, being a widowed workaholic, had gone without for too many years. "That's one reason I keep it short."

She drew her fingers down to trace his jaw and he dropped his gaze from her eyes to her soft pink lips. Her bottom lip was curved and plump, and the upper was narrow and arched. The asymmetry of her mouth was as intriguing and beautiful as the rest of her. When she scraped her palm across two days' worth of beard stubble, her nostrils flared. And when her fingertips tugged slightly against him, he closed the distance between them and covered her mouth with his.

He lost himself in the feeling of Jessie's lips surrendering beneath his. He leisurely took his fill of her little grasps and nibbles, of her angling her mouth first one way, then another as she got acquainted with his kiss. With his pulse revving up and his desire spinning out of control, he stroked his tongue along the seam of her lips, and she parted for him. Garrett delved in to fully taste her for the first time. Her tongue was still minty from brushing her teeth the night before. Although her responses were gentle, there was no shyness to the rasp of her tongue sliding against his or the tips of her fingers clinging to his face and neck.

At the tiny whimper from her throat, he captured either side of her jaw between his hands and tunneled his fingers into her hair. He tilted her head back against the basket of his hands and leaned in to claim the passion freeing itself from the tight confines of her guarded personality. No nubile, desperate young woman like Isla Gardner could hold a candle to the measured release of Jessie Bennington's passion. The cautious beginning of this embrace only made the gift of opening up and sharing herself with him that much more precious. What she demanded, he gave. What he asked for, she returned to him tenfold.

About the time Garrett became aware of the pressure swelling behind his zipper, he had the idea that patience might be a better course for this newfound closeness than laying her down on the bed and stabbing his palms against the tight points of her breasts that poked to attention through the cotton of her shirt. And about the time that thought made him ease back from her beautiful mouth, Jessie slipped her fingers between their lips and abruptly pushed him away.

"That was a nice *good morning*." His tone was embarrassingly breathless as he smiled his thanks and pleasure. "I could wake up like this every day."

Oh, hell. This was more than her coming to her senses before he could. That was panic in her eyes. Her pink, kiss-swollen lips spoke of shared passion, but her pale skin and eyes, which seemed to focus everywhere around the room except on him, sent a message of uncertainty and maybe even regret.

He rested his hand on her knee. "Jessie?" She jerked her leg away from him and hugged her knees up to her chest. Maybe she didn't understand what she'd done for him last night, that he wasn't expecting anything more from her right now. "That's the best I've slept in a long time. My body seemed to naturally relax, knowing you were here with me. I could touch you, and I didn't worry or wonder about anything. I felt…safe… with you beside me."

Her nod said she understood, maybe even felt the same way. But her words said something else. "Shadow needs to go outside." She patted the bed beside her, as if she'd just now realized the two of them were alone. "Where's Shadow?"

"He's fine. He got through the night without any

issues. I already put him out. He's downstairs eating breakfast now."

"I need to check—"

"No, you don't. We've already walked the perimeter to make sure there are no new tire tracks, and I've talked with my staff. No sightings of a car matching the description of the one you caught on camera—and not enough of a plate number to positively identify the car's owner. You can talk to me for five minutes," he gently chided. "How did you sleep? Are you feeling stronger this morning?" He picked up her mug and handed it to her. "Drink your coffee before it gets cold."

"Fine. Yes." She looked down into the milky brown depths of the coffee. "Did you put cream and sugar in it?"

"Yes." That's right, he paid attention. He knew how ridiculously sweet she liked her coffee.

She set the mug back down without tasting the drink and stood to pace back and forth between the bed and the door. "You shouldn't have kissed me like that."

Garrett stayed where he was, hoping a calm voice and less intimidating silhouette would help her calm herself. "Why not? You seemed to enjoy it. I know I did."

"Of course, I did. I wouldn't have kissed you back if I felt pressured or I didn't like it. But I—"

"You shouldn't have plastered your body against mine all night and made me believe you like me." He caught her hand when she moved past him again. "We needed to hold each other last night. I'm okay with that. That kiss was just the punctuation to the need we shared."

"Garrett—"

"I know you feel the chemistry between us, too."

"No. No chemistry. We're friends. Period." She pulled her hand away and spoke firmly, as if saying it out loud made it so. At least she was making eye contact now. "Last night, I was vulnerable. I haven't been held like that for twelve years, and I needed you. Your strength. Your warmth. Just…solid you to hold on to. You helped me through a tough day, and I'm grateful. But that doesn't mean we're an item now. Just because you spent the night—"

"—in the same bed—"

"—doesn't mean we're dating. You don't even like me that way."

Garrett sprang to his feet. "The hell I don't. You think I sleep with every friend who's having a rough go of things? What do you think that kiss was about? I bring you that fancy coffee I can't stand three or four mornings a week just so I can sit on the front porch and spend time with you. I stayed with you yesterday well beyond my body's limits and the duties of my office because you needed me, and I was worried about you." She tipped her head back to hold his gaze but didn't retreat. "I. Like. You. A lot."

"Garrett—"

"I guess I don't know how you feel about me. I thought I did, but maybe I was wrong. I believed you were keeping me at arm's length to protect yourself, because you were still grieving for your husband, or you felt guilty about caring for another man, or you just don't want to risk getting hurt." Bingo. He felt her flinch like a punch to the gut. He blew out his anger and breathed in sadness, mourning the loss of what could be between them. "But don't tell me how *I* feel. I know exactly what my emotions are. How much I'm attracted to you, how I love to see your smile. How you make me laugh, how much I admire you for all you've accomplished. How much I want to kiss your beautiful mouth again. I can keep my distance for now if that's what you want. If that's what it takes for you to get comfortable with me being in your life. But make no mistake, I *am* in your life. And until you tell me you don't feel anything at all for me, I'm not going anywhere. I will never be dishonest with you. I was hoping you could do the same for me."

"Garrett, I can't… You want honesty? I lost *everything* once. And it broke me. It has taken me twelve years and a therapy dog to get to where I am now. I can't do that again." She reached out but didn't touch him. "You deserve a woman who can give you her heart and her body and a family and forever. As much as a part of me might want to be that woman—I'm not. I'm damaged goods. And I don't just mean I can't give you children."

"You're not…" But he didn't finish the argument. If that was what she believed, then he wasn't going to change her mind by arguing with her. Instead, he plowed his fingers through his hair and tried to let her know that he understood how hard it was to find and trust a new relationship later in life, especially after surviving a tragedy the way she had. "After Haley, I wasn't sure I could love again, either. My heart felt all used up. Then I met you, chasing down that stupid stray dog, and I wanted to try." She had to understand this wasn't a fling for him, that nothing he felt for her was casual. "I still want to try."

Confusion was stamped on her face as she hugged herself tightly. He wanted to take her in his arms and shield her from the stress she was obviously feeling. But he didn't. She didn't want him to, and he would respect that.

"I don't want to give you false hope. I care about you too much to want to be the woman who hurts you." Her words were painfully sincere.

"What if you're the woman who makes me happy? Hell, Jessie, I'm a patient man. But you've got to give us a chance."

She shook her head. "You're easy to love, Garrett. But that also means you *won't* be easy to lose."

Now he did reach for her. He needed the connection. He feathered his fingers into her loose waves and brushed her hair behind her ear. "You're not going to lose me."

"You wear a gun and a badge, Garrett. You deal with violence on some level every day of your life. I'm not sure I can live with that."

Now the flashback this morning made sense. Eloise had trained her gun on *him*. Whether or not she realized it, Jessie had reacted because on some level, she already cared for him—and she'd thought she was going to lose him.

"I can't give up my job, Jess."

"I would never ask you to."

"I've got another fifteen years before they force me to retire. It'll end up being more of a desk job by then. But I love doing what I do."

"And you're good at it." She laid her hand over his where it rested against the side of her neck. "I'm not asking you to wait for me to be whole again. I may never be. I'm telling you to move on."

"No." Not an option for him. He was going to fight for them even if she couldn't. "Jessie—honey—you are stronger than you know. Look at all the people you help. Look at the animals you've helped. You run a successful business—and don't think I don't know that some of it's charitable work. Look at how far you've come. On your own."

She let go and moved away to count off perceived shortcomings on her fingers. "Flashbacks? Bawling when my dog gets sick? Screwing up the best kiss I've had in years?"

At least they were on the same page with the physical connection they shared. "You didn't screw up a damn thing. And Shadow is more than your dog. I'd be worried if you didn't lose it a little bit."

"If that's how I reacted to his diagnosis, how do you think I'm going to react if something happens to you?"

Garrett inhaled deeply. She couldn't see what was so clear to him. "You might cry. You might use a friend's shoulder to lean on. But then you'd suck it up and get on with living. You're like me in that respect. You get the job done. Because you have to. It may not be pretty. It may not be easy. But you do it. And hopefully, there's someone kind and caring and supportive around to help you do it."

Her eyes looked hopeful, although he could tell she was trying to come up with another argument to chase him out of her life. Thank goodness he wasn't some impatient young buck who moved on to the next pretty thing when the woman he really wanted proved to be a challenge. Convincing Jessie to take a chance on loving him might not be easy, but she was so worth the fight.

But he had to table the fight for now. His phone rang and her cell dinged with a text on the nightstand just a few seconds later.

He pulled his phone from his pocket and read the number. "Sorry. This is work." He crossed to the relative privacy of the guest room across the hall. "Deputy Caldwell." His morning went from bad to worse as he listened to his officer share the details about a county-wide search for two missing children.

By the time he'd hung up, Jessie stood in the doorway, holding up her phone. "I got an Amber Alert." The public notice she'd received would have been brief and to the point. "Two children?"

"Yeah. Runaways from Kansas City." Garrett suited up while he talked, tucking in his black T-shirt and strapping his protective vest over his chest. Then he pulled on his uniform shirt and buttoned it as he returned to her bedroom to retrieve his belt, gun, and badge. "The whole county is on notice. No clue where they went. The father didn't report them missing until this morning."

"How long have they been missing?" Jessie followed,

sounding stronger and looking less pale now that the conversation was centered on something other than him and her and the relationship she wasn't ready for. "Does your office know what happened?"

"They haven't shown up at school for three days. They alerted the father."

"Three days? And he just now reported it? Is there a mother in the picture? Did he think the children were with her?"

He shook his head. "Apparently, she died three years ago. Drug overdose. Dad has custody."

"Is there a relative? A sitter?"

He adjusted his belt at his waist and secured his holster at his hip before heading downstairs. "KCPD has checked all known connections with no luck. Official report says they got on the bus to school, but never reported to their classrooms."

"Why would they run away?"

"That's the million-dollar question. They're from a low-income neighborhood and money's tight. They're on the free meal program at school, and teachers reported that they sometimes wear clothes that they've outgrown. But they do well in their classes, and the dad is holding down a job as a delivery driver. They don't have a history of running."

"He must be out of his mind with worry." Her hands settled on her stomach and his heart wept for the baby she had lost. An incident like this was probably a nightmare trigger for her. "Do you think they were taken?"

That was every cop's worst fear. "Two children that young don't just disappear."

"I hope they're okay."

"Me, too. These are always the worst calls. Human trafficking or the death of a child? They're the hardest cases for me to handle." He grabbed his hat off the hall tree and headed to the front door. "I need to help find them."

Jessie hurried down the stairs behind him. "Do you want some breakfast before you go?"

"No."

"But I kept you up so late. You haven't even been home yet."

"I have a clean uniform at the sheriff's station. I'll shower there."

"I'm just trying to help. It's what a friend would do." She sounded a little lost. She was probably replaying every word he'd said to her and trying to figure out where she stood with him now. "I'm guessing that's not what you want from me."

He needed to get to the station to see where they stood on the search, coordinate with KCPD, and call in all available staff to help—and reassure them that even though seventy-two hours missing generally didn't bode well for the victims, they weren't giving up until they were found. The reasons why and gathering evidence as to any foul play would come later. Right now, priority one was locating the two reported runaways.

But then he remembered that as strong and tough as Jessie was on the outside, there was a vulnerable woman underneath who'd desperately needed the warmth of his body and the shelter of his arms last night. He could use a little tenderness and support right now, himself.

Garrett turned to her, snaked his hand around the back of her neck, and kissed her soundly, thoroughly, and far too quickly. He still cupped her nape gently and rested his forehead against hers. Her eyes tilted up to his, and he covered her hand resting against his chest. "I can't turn off how I feel about you, Jessie. You let me in last night, and it's hard for me to step back and pretend it never happened. But I hope you still trust me, that if you need me again, you'll call. About Shadow or Miss Eloise or late-night visitors or anything. I'll try to dial it back a notch so we can still be friends, so I can still see you and be a part of your life."

"You would do that? Even if it's only coffee on the porch in the mornings?"

"Even if it's only that. Look, I admit that I'm a workaholic. But I'm at an age where I've decided I need… want more than that." He released her to touch her hair and smooth the long waves down her back. "You're the most interesting, intriguing thing that's happened to me since Hayley died. I look forward to seeing you, discovering what we might laugh about—or argue about—next. I care about something beyond work now. I'm… *alive* again with you. I don't want to lose that."

"You are a grown, virile man. You need more than I can give you."

He shook his head. "I just need *you*. Maybe one day you'll believe it's safe to risk your heart on me. I'll keep it safe. I promise. I won't cheat. I will never lay a hand on you in anger. I'll do everything in my power to give you what you want, and more importantly, what you need." He pulled her hands from his chest and retreated a step. "But if that never happens, I want you to know that you're still safe with me. I'll still help you keep those mutts safe. I'll still be your friend."

"I don't deserve that kind of promise, Garrett."

"Yeah, you do." He lowered his head to press a quick kiss to her lips. He acknowledged the urge to claim those lips the way he had earlier, to show her exactly how good they could be together, that she was anything but *damaged goods* in his eyes. But this wasn't the right time. She wasn't ready for that. She might never be. So, he pulled away.

He put on his hat and strode out the front door. He had work to do.

GARRETT CROSSED HIS arms over his chest as he stood at the one-way mirror outside the interview room at KCPD's Fourth Precinct office. Since he was coordinating the search for the children listed as missing in this morning's Amber Alert outside the KC city limits, he'd been invited in to observe the most recent interview of the children's father, Zane Swiegert.

The guy looked understandably rough after finding out his son and daughter had disappeared. His clothes were wrinkled and stained, and he needed a shave. He'd been tearing up and his nose was running from the times he'd broken down during the interview. Although he and Hayley hadn't been blessed with children, Garrett knew he'd struggle to deal with it if someone he was responsible for—someone he loved—was harmed or taken. He thought back to yesterday when Jessie had suffered that flashback. He'd wanted to fix it for her, make whatever frightened her so go away. He was desperate to help, to protect, to take care of her. He hated feeling helpless.

Maybe Zane Swiegert felt helpless, too.

But his years in law enforcement left him feeling more suspicion than sympathy for Daddy Swiegert. The man was hiding something. Maybe it was as simple as being a lousy father and feeling guilty for losing track of his own children. Or maybe it was something more sinister.

Someone knew where those children were. Someone knew what had happened to them. Was it Swiegert?

The detectives interviewing Swiegert asked him to retrace his children's steps the morning they'd gone missing. He'd gotten them up for school and walked them out to the bus stop where they'd been picked up for school. They ate breakfast at school. Nate Swiegert was in the third grade; his younger sister, Abby, was in kindergarten. Yes, he knew the name of Nate's teacher, although he couldn't seem to come up with the name of his daughter's teacher. After school, they were supposed to walk over to a friend's apartment and stay with him until Zane got back from driving his delivery route late that night.

But none of those details were what pinged on Garrett's radar as he studied the relatively nondescript, brown-haired, blue-eyed man in his midthirties. Swiegert wore a small, bright white cast on his left hand, indicating he'd broken some fingers. Very recently. Maybe he'd punched a wall out of anger, guilt, or frustration. Or he'd been distracted and overtired and gotten into some kind of accident—shut his hand in a car door or put it through a window. Plus, the guy was sweating. Inside an air-conditioned building on a mild spring day, he was sweating.

Swiegert seemed even hazier recounting his own movements since the last time he'd seen his son and daughter. He'd driven his route that day but didn't show up for work yesterday. He said he'd called in sick with the flu, but his supervisor never got such a call. Why didn't he pick up his children at the friend's home? Because he was sick. How did he injure his fingers? At work. But you didn't go to work, the detectives reminded him. Then he got angry and sobbed again. Why were the cops grilling him and not out combing the streets for Nate and Abby?

A shadow fell over Garrett, and he turned to the tall, lanky man wearing a suit and tie who stepped up beside him. "You think he's faking it?" Detective Conor Wildman looked more like an up-and-coming executive at a Fortune 500 company than a WITSEC agent turned KCPD detective. He had been the one to call Garrett in from the sheriff's office in Lee's Summit. "I know I'd be out of my mind if anything happened to my daughter or wife. But there's something else going on with this guy, if you ask me."

"The tears? The sweat?" Garrett shrugged. "I think he's in legitimate pain. Though it's not all about his kids. Either the painkillers he was given for that hand have worn off…or he's going through withdrawal."

"Then your suspicions are the same as mine. I'm guessing he was off someplace getting high when his children went missing. It took him three days to sober up and realize they were gone." Wildman handed Garrett a file folder to read. "That's Swiegert's rap sheet. Wouldn't be the first time he's used cocaine."

"Or else the drugs are how he's coping with the stress. You do a tox screen?"

"Bad PR to lean too heavily on the parent until the kids are found."

Garrett skimmed the file. Drug possession arrests. Petty crimes to support his habit. "How did that guy keep custody of his children?"

"He was clean for a while after a mandatory stint in rehab following his wife's overdose. Kept his nose clean long enough to maintain a steady job and get his kids out of the foster system."

"So, this guy is a loser who doesn't deserve those kids. But he loves them, and they love him, and he's trying as hard as he can to stay clean or at least use less. So, the State and KCPD are doing all they can to reunite them?" He handed the file back to Detective Wildman. "Why am I here to listen to his sob story? Either something happened to them three days ago, they were taken and are long gone by now, or they ran away of their own volition. In which case, they've been surviving on the streets or out in the elements. None of that is good."

"I'm not affiliated with the missing persons' case, Deputy." That piqued his interest. "I'm part of a drug task force trying to take down a major player here in KC—Kai Olivera."

Garrett nodded. "I know the name. Second-generation American gangster living the dream in the big city. Human trafficking. Drugs. Small arms smuggling. I've made traffic stops on the highway where we've intercepted a couple of his cross-country shipments. I'm sure some of our locals who like to indulge themselves have bought his product off the streets. Is Zane Swiegert a customer of his?"

"He has been on and off for a few years." Wildman turned away from the interview to face Garrett. "My intel says Swiegert is driving for him now, too. He's using his delivery job to make drops and pick up payments from Olivera's people on the streets."

This scenario just got worse and worse. "So, Daddy Dearest is a scumbag who doesn't deserve those kids when we do find them." He refused to say *if* the children were found. "Why am I here? Arrest him already, and let me get back to work."

"We think Swiegert is key to bringing down Olivera."

"He's not going to testify against his supplier and employer." Although if there was any hint that he might, it could explain the damage done to his fingers—and why he seemed more nervous about the police asking so many questions than he was worried about his kids. "You think Olivera took the kids to leverage Swiegert into keeping his mouth shut?"

"I've got an undercover operative in Olivera's organization. While Olivera isn't above recruiting underage girls into his human trafficking business, my man hasn't seen or heard of anyone as young as elementary-school-age children being lured in with the promise of drugs, family, or money."

"That's a relief. Of sorts. Still doesn't put us any closer to finding those children." Garrett knew there had to be more to this conversation than idle specu-lation. Conor Wildman wanted something from him. "What is this meeting really about?"

The detective glanced around before ushering Gar-rett out of the interview watch room and over to the empty meeting room next door. "Zane Swiegert isn't the only witness who could talk to us about Olivera's activities. My inside man has spotted Olivera and one of his lieutenants entering Zane Swiegert's apartment building on more than one occasion. While Nate and Abby were present."

Garrett swore. "The children? You want them to tes-tify against that scumbag?"

"If Zane Swiegert thinks they have to—"

"He'd cooperate with KCPD to protect his children." Garrett shook his head. Kai Olivera might be the worst of the worst and needed to be taken down. But to ask a third grader or kindergartner to testify against him…? "That's a mighty big risk you'd be taking."

"When I say Kai Olivera is bad news, I'm being nice." Detective Wildman's flair for sarcasm was ob-vious. "I need someone to find those children and put them into protective custody at a safe house before we move on Olivera." Wildman pulled out a chair and sat. "A tip from the Amber Alert Hotline said two children matching Nate and Abby Swiegert's descriptions were spotted the morning they went missing getting on a public transit bus headed east out 40 Highway. Into your neck of the woods."

Public transit didn't come out as far as Lone Jack where he lived. But if they took it to the end of the line and got out, they could hike or, God forbid, hitchhike to get farther out of the city. "So KCPD is focusing their search east of the city in Jackson County."

Detective Wildman nodded. "Your jurisdiction."

Garrett pulled his ball cap from his back pocket and sat in the chair across from Wildman. "I've had a rash of break-ins and petty thefts the past three days. My money was on teenage vandals. But it could be the kids stealing supplies or finding a relatively warm spot to stay for the night."

"You looking into those?"

"I was until the Amber Alert took precedence." Maybe the string of random crimes did make sense if he put them into the right context. "Has information from the tip line gone out to the press? Would them heading east be public knowledge?"

The detective nodded. "Our information officer updates the public so they can assist with the search."

"What kind of car does Swiegert drive?"

The detective arched an eyebrow. "That's random."

"Not really."

Conor pulled up his phone and looked it up. "An old-model Ford Bronco." So not the lit-up Dodge Charger that had shown up at Jessie's ranch yesterday evening.

"What about Olivera? Anybody in your investigation drive a shiny new Dodge Charger fitted with underglow lights?"

Conor shook his head. "But this crew gets new vehicles all the time. Part of it is because they modify them to transport their coke and pot. Once we ID one of them, that vehicle is retired and torn apart at a chop shop. And part of it is just because Olivera and his crew have got a ton of money to spend. Are you going to explain that question to me?"

Garrett scrubbed his fingers through his hair. "Just some unexplained traffic in my part of the world. We may not be the only ones looking for those kids."

"Any sign of Kai Olivera?"

"A residential security camera caught a couple of vehicles where they shouldn't be. The images weren't clear enough to make an ID." He purposely left Jessie's name out of the conversation since she valued her privacy so much. "Are you familiar with K-9 Ranch?"

"That lady who trains protection and companion dogs?" Detective Wildman nodded. "She's done some good work for victims of violent crime. Our police psychologist, Dr. Kilpatrick, sent an officer who was struggling with PTSD to her."

"That lady is good friend of mine."

"That's where the car was sighted?"

Garrett nodded. "And you believe Swiegert is tied to Olivera?"

"I'm certain of it."

He was already on his feet and pulling out his phone to text Jessie to make sure she was okay, that there hadn't been any other unusual incidents at her place.

"Caldwell." Garrett stopped in the doorway at Detective Wildman's harsh tone. "Are we on the same page here? If you find those kids, I want to be the first person you call. Not the search team, not Family Services. I need to know they're safe and off the playing field so I can put the pressure on Swiegert and nail Olivera."

"You'll be the first call I make."

Chapter Six

Jessica looked up from the A. L. Baines fantasy novel she was reading and wondered what the dogs out in the kennels were going on about now. So much barking. She knew sometimes it was a chain reaction type of thing—one dog saw or smelled or heard something, and all the others chimed in. But after the recent break-ins and mysterious late-night visitors she'd had, she wondered if there could be something more to it.

Although, anyone who tried to break into a place with so many dogs was either stupid or seriously desperate. *Seriously desperate.* That sounded dangerous. She couldn't be amused by her dogs' doglike behavior if there was someone dangerous out there.

After slipping a bookmark between the pages, she set aside her book and woke up her laptop that she'd brought to the coffee table to pay some bills earlier. She pulled up the camera feeds outside. Nothing at the front gate. But since her phone hadn't pinged, she hadn't expected to see anything suspicious there, anyway.

She watched a couple of minutes of the camera feed from the barn. No strange cars. No Soren Hauck. No faceless strangers. But something was out there. Even

with the grainy nighttime images of black and white
and gray, she could make out several of her charges
pawing at their gates at the front of their kennels. Ras-
cal had his little black nose poking through the chain
links, and Jasper had his big jowls pressed against his
gate to get a closer look at whatever the other dogs had
seen. Even her eleven-month-old pit bull, Baby, was at
her gate, her whole body bouncing with every bark.

Was that...?

Jessica pulled the computer onto her lap and replayed
the last few seconds. There was a ghost of movement,
something darker than the rest of the shadows that
darted around the corner of the kennel and disappeared
into the camera's blind spot at the far end of the building.
Whatever she'd seen was low to the ground, small and
quick. Skunk? Raccoon? Someone's feet? She shook her
head at the fanciful reminder of the witch's feet curling
up and disappearing in *The Wizard of Oz*. Her heart rate
sped up a notch, but she instantly felt Shadow's head
resting atop her thigh.

"I'm okay, buddy," she reassured him, and thanked
him with a rub beneath his collar. "That scene in the
movie always freaks me out a little bit." She tried to
freeze the image, but it was just a blob of shadow
among the shadows. "I don't know what that was."
She sat back and watched the dogs still barking at the
disturbance that seemed to have scuttled out of there,
at least from this angle. "If this is going to be a thing
out here, maybe I'd better invest in more cameras. I've
got too many blind spots."

She was beginning to understand Garrett's frustration with an unsolved mystery. Replaying the image again, she realized that whatever had cast that shadow never appeared on screen. It was as if it had started to come around the end of the kennels, then darted back to its hidey-hole when it saw the reception of twelve dogs waiting for him. Waiting for *it*? She glanced up. Was *it* still out there? She'd locked the front and back doors, hadn't she? Jessica exhaled a deep breath, forcing herself to relax. Of course, she'd locked the doors. She kept them locked whether she was inside the house or out with the dogs, and certainly when she left the ranch. And she'd double-checked them after letting Shadow out that last time after dinner, before she'd picked up her book and laptop and curled up beneath the throw blanket on her couch.

She watched Toby bound through the camera feed and disappear after the blur of movement she'd seen. That wasn't anything much to worry about. Toby had two speeds—fast and playful, and flat on his belly to lounge or sleep. She'd seen him chase after autumn leaves floating through the air, so his pursuit of *it* wasn't necessarily cause for alarm.

But where was Rex? Apparently, whatever had stirred up the others was beneath his interest. That calmed her a little. He was the true guard dog of the ranch, and if he wasn't worried, she wouldn't be, either. Soon enough, the barking outside subsided into the quiet night air, and she saw the dogs settle down into their beds or go back to a late-night snack in their kennels.

Jessica reached over to pet Shadow, who was stretched out on the sofa beside her. She always loved the warmth that came off his body and relished the way he stretched and rolled beneath her hand so she could scratch just the right places to make him feel better, too. "Well, that was a big hullabaloo. But if you think we're okay, then I'll think that, too."

She set the laptop back on the coffee table and checked the time on her phone. She should make herself get up and go to bed, only, she had a feeling sleep would be elusive tonight. Too many fears and memories had been stirred up in the past forty-eight hours for her to trust that she wouldn't have nightmares or that Shadow wouldn't have another seizure. The only time she'd been able to truly stop the worries and feel safe was when she'd plastered herself to the heat and strength of Garrett's body last night. She had a feeling that wasn't going to happen again anytime soon. Not after her panicked reaction this morning. Too much had happened between them too fast for her brain and her trust to keep up. She knew she had feelings for him, but risking the hard-won stability in her life was a mighty big ask. He promised to be patient with her, but was that fair to Garrett? He was a mature, accomplished, sexy man. He deserved a woman who could be his equal—not one he had to *be patient with* and take care of. He'd already gone through that with his late wife and her battle with cancer. Jessica's issues were emotional, not physical, but that didn't mean she wouldn't be a burden rather than a help to him.

Before setting down her phone, Jessica glanced to see if she'd had any more texts from Garrett. He'd checked in with her midmorning, telling her he'd showered and shaved and eaten a breakfast burrito, so she didn't have to worry about him not taking care of himself. She'd sent back a smiley face and assured him she was fine and not to worry about her. She'd worked with two clients today and put all her dogs through some kind of training exercise—as normal a day for her as she could ask for.

Around five o'clock, he'd updated her on the search for the missing children. No leads. No luck. Allegedly, they'd taken a bus east on 40 Highway until the route ended. After that, who knew? There were so many highways crossing through Kansas City, that if someone had picked up the children, they could be several states away in any direction by now. KCPD had some suspicion about the father, since he'd waited so long to report them missing.

She sensed there was something he wasn't telling her. But she assumed it was related to the investigation, and that he couldn't share information about the case. All she knew was that it was all hands on deck in the search for those runaways, and that Garrett would exhaust every skill and connection he had until they were found. When she expressed her sympathy for the father, Garrett had replied with a cryptic response about Mr. Swiegert having trouble of his own to deal with.

Jessica had answered with a brief text saying if there was any mystery to be solved, she was sure he would figure it out. The children were the priority right now, not proving whether or not the father had committed any crime, or if he should at least be reported to Family Services. He'd answered with a single thumbs-up emoji and gone silent for the rest of the evening.

It would be another late night for Garrett, and she felt guilty that she'd misled him and made him so angry this morning. Had he eaten lunch? Dinner? A true friend would fix him a sandwich or grab a to-go meal and take it to him at the sheriff's office.

So why hadn't she done that already?

Probably because she knew deep down inside that there was something more than friendship between them. Garrett might be brave enough to embrace the possibilities, but she was not. It scared the daylights out of her to admit that she'd been falling in love with Garrett Caldwell for some time now.

Maybe she wasn't ready to give her heart to anyone. But she could do better by him than she had this morning. "Do the right thing, woman," she encouraged herself out loud. Shadow flicked his ears as if he agreed. "Bossy."

She pulled up Garrett's number and typed out a text.

Jessica: I'm sorry about this morning. In case it wasn't clear, I'm grateful for everything you did for me yesterday and last night. I'm okay now. Don't worry about me. I don't want my hang-ups to distract you from doing your job or taking care of yourself.

His answer came through almost immediately.

Garrett: Can't promise I won't worry about you.

Jessica: No. Focus on those kids. They need you more than I do.

When he didn't immediately reply, she sent another text.

Jessica: Not to sound like an old nag, but have you eaten anything since that burrito? Put your feet up for ten minutes and rested your eyes?

Garrett: No and no. But it's nice to have someone worry about me.

Jessica: I never promised I wouldn't worry about you, either. ;)

Garrett: Okay if I bring you coffee in the morning?

Jessica: I'd like that. I will consider everything you said. I can't make any promises, though.

Garrett: That gives me hope.

Another text followed moments later.

Garrett: And fair warning… I will be kissing you again. I need that connection.

Jessica: That's your idea of being patient with me?

Garrett: Did you miss the part about me saying I needed
you? It's been a tough day.

How could a text convey such exhaustion and frustration? The woman she'd once been before tragedy
had irrevocably changed her would have reached out
to offer comfort and strength. Hell, the woman she was
now wanted to do that for Garrett. She wanted to be
what he needed. She wanted to be the woman he could
depend on. She wanted to be enough.

Jessica: Okay. One kiss.

She smiled at his answer.

Garrett: I'll take it.

It wasn't fair, but she felt a little lighter at the idea of
seeing Garrett tomorrow morning. She was even tamping down anticipation at kissing him again. Would it
be one of those quick, branding kisses where he held
the back of her neck and made her feel surrounded and
cherished by him? Or one of those toe-curling seduc-
tions like she'd woken up to this morning, where she'd
momentarily forgotten her name as well as all the reasons why she wasn't a good bet for a relationship?

Jessica started to text him good-night and wish him
luck on his team's search, but Shadow suddenly hopped
up on all four legs and nudged his nose through the
curtains to look out over the front porch. "Now what?"

A split second later, she heard Rex's deep woof.

She hadn't gotten any notification on her phone that someone had driven onto the property, but she trusted Shadow's and Rex's instincts more than she trusted computer electronics when it came to security.

She pulled up her computer screen in time to see Rex chasing Toby out of the barn. That was weird. The only time she'd seen Rex turn on his patrol buddy was when Toby had been pestering the Anatolian's adopted goats. Jessica tapped Shadow's shoulder to bring his attention back to her. "Do we need to check this out?"

The rangy German shepherd mix jumped down and made a beeline for the back door.

"Give me a minute," Jessica chided, reaching for her lace-up boots. By the time she pulled on her denim barn coat and tucked her keys, phone, and flashlight into its roomy pockets, Shadow was scratching furiously at the door.

For a split second, she wondered if she should call Garrett or even 9-1-1 to report the commotion after so many destructive incidents happening on her and other farms in the area. But if she was tired, he had to be beyond exhausted. She didn't need him to come to her rescue again. Especially if this turned out to be nothing more than a raccoon in the barn or Toby trying to play with the goats again.

Jessica locked the door behind her and texted Garrett.

Jessica: Sorry to cut this short. Dogs are going off. Don't see anything on the cameras. Checking it out.

Garrett: Wait. I'm in the city right now. I can be there in twenty minutes.

Jessica: I have a dozen dogs to back me up. I'll be fine.

She turned on her flashlight, confirmed there were no unfamiliar vehicles in her drive, and nothing big like a deer or bobcat or neighbor with a shotgun wandering too close to her facilities. No, whatever had made Rex cranky enough to scoot Toby out of the barn probably wasn't a threat to her.

But there *was* a threat.

When she heard Shadow growling, she took off at a run to reach him in the barn. Once she got inside, she flipped on the lights and tried to make sense of what she was seeing. Shadow, the old man of the ranch and undisputed leader of the pack, was crouched down in the dirt in front of Penny and her puppies' stall. Oh, no. Had a fox or coyote gotten in and gone after one of the pups? If so, why wasn't Mama Penny going crazy? And what was Rex carrying in his mouth as he trotted back to his home with the goats?

"Shadow?" Jessica slowly approached the dog, knowing when he was tense and on guard like this, it was wise not to startle him. "Shadow." She called out more forcefully. When he looked up at her, she motioned him to her side. She grabbed hold of his collar and inhaled a steadying breath, bracing herself for a predator or carnage or whatever the dogs had cornered in the barn. Flipping her flashlight to arm herself with a club if necessary, she released Shadow, slid open the stall gate, and stared right into the tines of her own pitchfork. She retreated half a step. "Oh, my."

The little boy wielding that pitchfork had blue eyes, dirty, disheveled brown hair and a fist-sized bruise at the corner of his mouth. "Leave us alone!" he warned. "We're not hurtin' anybody."

Us? She raised her hands in the universal sign for surrender as she leaned a little to one side to spot a small, blond-haired girl in the straw, curled up beneath the missing blanket from her storage room. A bobtail Australian shepherd puppy was snugged in her arms. Penny seemed to be okay with these children in the stall with her puppies. She seemed familiar with them, knew they weren't a threat.

Jessica brought her gaze back to the boy who was so staunchly defending the little girl. "Did you break into my storage room last night?" She remembered the indentation in the straw. "Did you sleep here?"

He pulled his narrow shoulders back. "I didn't steal your blanket," he insisted, glancing down at the sleeping girl. "It's right there."

"I don't mind that you borrowed it. You're taking care of her."

"Abby's sick. I was looking for medicine." Some of the defiance leaked out of the boy's tone and posture. "She was so cold, she was shivering." He sounded scared and tired, and had clearly been smacked hard enough to leave that bruise, but the pitchfork never wavered. "I'm sorry I broke your jar. I gave the treats to your dogs so they wouldn't bark at us all the time."

"That was smart." Jessica's praise seemed to quiet

his fear a little bit. "I hope you didn't cut yourself on all that broken glass."

He gave his head a sharp shake.

"Are *you* warm enough?" she asked. The sleeves of his denim jacket didn't reach his wrists, and he wore only a thin T-shirt underneath. "I could get another blanket for you."

"I'm okay," he insisted. "I have to stay awake to protect Abby."

Jessica's heart nearly broke at this boy's staunch defense of the little girl. She suspected there was a whole lot of backstory she was missing here. But the reasons behind their rough condition and hiding out in her barn didn't matter. She needed to get that weapon out of his hands and get them both the help they needed. She just had to keep talking until she could get the boy to relax, sort of the way she'd calm a skittish dog to earn his trust. She pointed her head toward the far end of the barn, where Rex had gone. "Rex is that big dog. He doesn't like a lot of people. But the fact that he took a treat from you means you're good with dogs. He knows you're an okay guy."

"He wouldn't let me pet him."

"Nah. He's not into that. He's happier hanging out with his goat friends." She glanced down at Shadow sitting beside her. "Would you like to pet a dog?"

His blue eyes widened. "He growled at me."

"Because he was protecting me. Just like you're protecting Abby." She stroked the top of Shadow's head. "He won't hurt anyone unless I tell him to, and I would never do that."

This boy was such a thinker, evaluating his options. He looked to be about eight or nine, just a few years younger than her own child would be now if he'd survived. But he seemed old beyond his years. "I wanted to pet the puppies, but I read that you aren't supposed to handle puppies too much when they're still with their mom."

"That's right." She was starting to make some progress. He was carrying on a conversation now. "Do you like to read?" He nodded. "I've got a ton of books in my house. Would you like to see them?"

"Mrs. Furkin said I shouldn't go anywhere with a stranger."

"Who's Mrs. Furkin?" A babysitter who was missing her charges, she hoped.

"My teacher. I'm in the third grade."

He didn't get his advice from a parent? Some other family member? Jessica knew she was about to say and do a few things that most children were taught to ignore to keep them safe from a stranger. "Is Abby your sister?" He nodded. "I'm Jessie. Jessie Bennington." She wasn't quite sure why she'd used the name Garrett called her, but it seemed friendlier, easier to pronounce. "What's your name?"

He hesitated for a moment, as if debating whether or not it was safe to answer. "Nate."

No last name. But she'd work with whatever the boy gave her. Without moving any closer, she risked putting her hands down. "You're not going to poke me with that thing, are you?" He leaned the pitchfork against the wall of the stall but kept his hand on it. That was probably as much of a welcome as he was going to give her right now. Jessica inched closer. "May I check on Abby? See if she's sleeping okay?"

At least, she hoped the girl was just sleeping. Jessica's stomach clenched at the idea of the child suffering out here on the chilly spring night. She'd like to get in there to see just how ill the little girl was. She looked to be about five or six. How long had they been out in the elements like this? Did Abby need to see a doctor?

"Nate, I'm going to show you something." Using her hands and a clear voice, she gave Shadow a series of commands. "Sit. Down. Stay." Shadow's tongue lolled out the side of his mouth and she knew he was relaxing now that the pitchfork had been set aside and she wasn't being threatened. Then she held out a hand to the boy. "Come here, Nate. See how relaxed Shadow's ears are? Curl your fingers into a fist like this." She showed him what she wanted him to do. "Now hold it close to his nose and let him sniff you. He'll realize you're Rex's friend, and that Penny isn't worried about you being around her puppies. Dogs use their noses more than anything to learn about their world. Once he's familiar with your scent, he'll let you pet him. In fact, I bet he'd really like it if you would."

Although he avoided touching her hand, Nate knelt in the straw near Shadow and let the dog sniff his fist. When the dog slurped his tongue over the boy's fingers, Nate jerked back and landed on his butt in the straw. "I thought he was gonna bite me."

Jessica smiled and petted Shadow. "No. That means he likes you."

"He does?"

"Sure. It's a puppy kiss." She curtailed her instinct to reach for Nate and help him move closer. Instead, she demonstrated how Shadow liked to be petted. "Try again. Like this." Nate almost smiled as he petted the top of Shadow's head without incident. "You may smell like the treats you handled. That's a good smell to him."

For the first time, a spark of excitement in Nate's voice made him sound like a true little boy. "Can I give him a treat?"

"You may."

Nate scrambled away to unzip his backpack and pulled out a beefy chew. To his credit, Shadow eagerly took the treat from the boy's hand and lay down to enjoy it while Nate petted him some more.

"Good boy, Shadow." She praised both the boy and the dog for handling this first meeting so well. While Nate was distracted with the dog, Jessica scooted across the straw to check on Abby. Even before she brushed aside her curly blond hair and touched the girl's skin, she could feel the heat radiating off her fragile body. The girl had a fever, and her skin was pale. She murmured her brother's name at Jessica's touch and rolled toward her, but didn't completely wake up. "How long has Abby been sick?"

"Since last night. She threw up the dog food I gave her."

Jessica thought *she* might be sick. They were eating the dog food? "When was the last time you ate? People food?"

"We tried to eat the eggs next door, but they were gross. I like 'em scrambled."

"I do, too. With some cinnamon toast and bacon. I've got all that in the house. I could make you some."

Nate remembered his charge and came over to kneel on the other side of his sister. "I'm not leaving Abby."

"I have food for her, too. What does she like to eat?"

"Cereal with marshmallows in it."

"Well, I don't have any of that. But maybe I have something else she'd like." She picked up the spotted puppy and set him back in his box with Mama Penny.

When she came back to smooth Abby's hair off her warm forehead, the little girl opened her eyes. "I like your puppies. I named that one Charlie. My best friend at school is named Charlie."

"That's a good name." She smiled down at the little girl, who seemed to be more trusting than her big brother. "My name is Jessie, and I'm here to help you. Is your tummy upset?"

Abby glanced over to her brother, then nodded. "I frowed up."

"That's okay. That's just your tummy trying to feel better."

Jessica felt she'd won them over enough to take charge a little more. She looked at Nate. "Has she had anything to drink today?"

"We drank some water from your hose. I put it in the water bottles we brought from home."

Between hose water and raw eggs, she had to wonder if the girl had picked up some kind of intestinal parasite. She mentally crossed her fingers that this was just a touch of the flu, or the manifestation of the girl's exhaustion and their sketchy diet. And as much as she wanted to ask them where *home* was, Jessica had a feeling she already knew the answer. Besides, getting these children fed and taken care of had just become priority one. "I'd like to take you both inside my house, where you can sleep in a real bed and eat some real food." She pulled out her cell phone and showed it to them. "I have a friend in the sheriff's department. He's the police outside of the city. May I call him? He could help you."

"No!" Nate slapped her hand and knocked the phone into the straw. "I don't want to go back to Kansas City. He'll hurt Abby."

"My friend Garrett won't hurt your sister."

His eyes widened with fear, and he moved between Jessie and his sister. "The bald man will."

"Who's the bald man?" Jessica shook her head and focused on priority one. The details as to why Nate was protecting Abby didn't matter right now. These children were frightened and needed food and help. "I don't know any bald man. He isn't here. My dogs wouldn't let him hurt you."

"If you make us go back, we'll run away again."

"I don't want you to go anywhere except inside my house, where I can help Abby and get you both someplace where it's warm and safe."

Abby whimpered between them. "Natey, I don't feel good. My tummy's empty."

"Can you make her better?"

"I can try." Jessica picked up her phone. "But I need

to call my friend. I won't let him take you anywhere. I need his help to take care of you."

"Natey, I want to sleep in a bed. It's itchy here." Abby reached out for her brother. "Can't the dog lady help us? She's not like Daddy's friend. She's nice."

So many questions to ask about what these two had been through. But Jessica held her tongue and waited for big brother to make his decision.

"It'll be okay, Abs." Nate squeezed his little sister's hand. "Jessie knows all about dogs and medicine. She's gonna take care of you."

"Thank you." Jessica wasn't about to correct the boy's mistaken assumption about her skill set, not if it got him to cooperate with her. Abby wore a sparkly pink tracksuit, but had no coat, so Jessica tucked the ratty blanket around her small form and scooped her up into her arms.

Abby curled into Jessica's chest. "You smell like flowers."

"Can you put your arms around my neck?" With a weak nod, the little girl slipped her grubby hands around the collar of Jessica's coat. She weighed less than some of the dogs she manhandled for baths or trips to the vet. "Nate, will you grab her book bag and bring it with us? Yours, too."

He dutifully picked up both their backpacks but hung back. "Can Shadow come with us?"

"He goes everywhere I go." Although Shadow was looking to her for his next command, she gave Nate the job instead. "Say his name, then 'Heel,' and tap your thigh. He'll fall into step beside you."

Jessica hurried out of the barn, ignoring the barking from the kenneled dogs. Behind her she heard a small voice, "Shadow. Heel. He did it!"

"Good man." She let her praise get both boy and dog moving. "Let's go."

Jessica carried Abby into the house and up the stairs to lay the girl on the bed in one of the guest rooms. Nate and Shadow trotted up the stairs right behind them. The boys stayed in the room with Abby as Jessica hurried into the main bathroom to retrieve a cool, damp washcloth and a thermometer. Nate hovered at the end of the bed, watching her every move as she tended to the girl. Abby's fever wasn't dangerously high, but she needed to cool down and get some fluids in her. And brave little Nate needed to eat.

She gave the girl a sponge bath of all her extremities, then removed her tennis shoes and tucked her beneath the covers. "Will you sit here and hold your sister's hand while I talk to my friend? Make sure she keeps the washcloth on her forehead. We need to get her fever down."

Nate took her place sitting beside his sister on the bed while she stepped away and pulled out her phone again. When she looked at her screen, she saw several messages from Garrett.

Garrett: Jess? Still there?

Garrett: You okay?

Garrett: I'm on my way.

Garrett: Jess?

She pulled up her keyboard and started to text him.

She looked into a pair of distrustful blue eyes and decided to call Garrett instead. Nate needed to hear what she was saying and not think she might be telling her deputy friend something other than what she'd promised.

"Jess?" He answered on the first ring. "Why didn't you answer me? There's been a development in the investigation. The kids' father may have some criminal ties. I need to you stay inside and keep things locked up."

"There's been a development here, too. Before you get here, stop and get me some children's acetaminophen and lemon-lime soda."

"What? Why?"

"I found your runaways."

Chapter Seven

"They doing okay?"

Jessica felt Garrett lean against the doorframe behind her as she watched Nate and Abby sleep in the guest bedroom across the hall from her own room. Abby was curled up in a ball around the doll she'd pulled from her backpack. It was missing a hunk of red yarn from one of its yellow ponytails. But she could tell it was well loved and had been played with and cuddled often. Nate, on the other hand, was spread out like a starfish on a pile of blankets and a sleeping bag on the floor. Her ever-faithful Shadow was stretched out on the pallet beside him. A night-light beside the bed and the light she'd left on in the hallway bathroom cast the only illumination on the second floor.

"For now. He ate everything I fixed for him. Man-sized portions. He's a starving growing boy." She glanced up at the real man beside her and found him staring at the children as intently as she had. "Abby ate the applesauce and some of the toast I gave her so the acetaminophen wouldn't upset her stomach. Thank you for bringing that. Her temperature's down below three digits already."

"Glad to do it." His voice was a low whisper against her ear. "Did they tell you anything more about what they've been through?"

She shook her head. "Abby doesn't say much, and Nate is pretty guarded. I think they've been in survival mode for so long, it'll be hard to earn their trust." She rubbed her hands up and down her arms, warding off an inner chill. "I'm half afraid they're going to bolt if I stop watching them."

His hand settled at the small of her back, sharing some of his warmth and reassurance. "I think they're taking their cues from the dogs. If Shadow and the others trust you, then maybe they can, too. At least a little bit. Any trouble getting them settled down?"

"I had them both take a bath. Then I started reading *The Phantom Tollbooth* to them. All Abby cared about was the picture of the dog with a clock in his belly. She dozed off in my lap. But Nate made it through two chapters before he admitted he was sleepy."

"He's a tough kid."

"Tougher than he needs to be at his age." Garrett made a soft sound of agreement in his throat. "I wanted to give them each their own room. She wouldn't even get in bed until Nate came in. I made him a pallet on the floor. He pulled it between the door and the bed. She didn't fall into a deep sleep until he lay down beside her and held her hand. He didn't give up until Shadow came in and lay down beside him."

"I can only think of one reason why he'd want to position himself between his sister and the door," Garrett grumbled.

"To protect her?" Garrett was practically vibrating when she nudged her shoulder against his. "Let's take the conversation downstairs." When Shadow raised his head to silently ask if he needed to go with her, she smiled and made it clear he was off duty for now. "Stay here, good boy. Relax." The dog laid his head back down on Nate's outstretched arm. It was probably the pallet he was enjoying, although she didn't think either the dog or the boy minded the company and warm body beside him.

Downstairs, Garrett peeked through the windows and checked the locks while she went to the kitchen to brew them a fresh pot of decaf coffee. He pulled out a stool at the island counter, braced his elbows on top, and scrubbed his fingers through his hair in that habit of his that indicated fatigue or frustration. Jessica's heart squeezed at the rumpled mess he left in its wake. As much as she wanted to go to him and straighten those sexy spikes of hair, she kept her fingers busy pouring their coffee. She set a steaming mug in front of him and doctored up her own drink before pulling out the stool beside him to sit.

She waited for him to sip some of the reviving brew before she voiced her own concerns. "What happened to those children? Nate said the 'bald man' wanted to hurt Abby. What scared them so badly that running away was their only option?"

"The 'bald man'?" Garrett glanced up from the drink he'd been studying. "Did they give you a name?"

"No."

"But you think they've seen him? Had contact with him?"

"Enough that they're deathly afraid of him. Were they talking about their father?"

Garrett set down his mug and pulled out his cell phone. "This is their father, Zane Swiegert."

She leaned over to look at the candid shot that had been taken through a window at a police station. Zane Swiegert looked like a taller, grown-up version of Nate with brown hair and blue eyes. But he also looked… wild.

Wild brown eyes.

Jessica squeezed her eyes shut and shook off the memory of her husband's murderer before a flashback could take hold. When she opened her eyes, she discovered that she'd latched on to Garrett's forearm, much the same way she reached for Shadow whenever she needed to anchor herself to reality.

"Jessie?" Garrett's hand closed gently over her own, warming it against the ink of his military tattoo. "What's wrong?"

She drummed up a wry smile but didn't pull away. "I'm okay. He just…" She inhaled a steadying breath. "With that unwashed, uncombed hair and the circles under his eyes, he reminds me of Lee Palmer."

"The man who killed your husband and shot you?"

She nodded. "Palmer was high on something when he came to our house that morning. Probably had to be to make sense of doing something so desperate. As if killing John and trying to kill me would get his wife or his children or his money back." She shifted her gaze from the picture up to Garrett's concerned expression. Although he'd shaved at some point during the day, she could see the dark, silver-studded stubble shading his jaw again. "Nate and Abby's father is using, isn't he. He has the same look."

"Yeah. Cocaine seems to be his drug of choice. I snapped that picture when he was in KCPD for questioning today. He sounded like he genuinely wants his kids. But there's something more going on there." After swiping the image off his phone, he leaned over to press a gentle kiss to her temple. "Sorry for dredging up bad memories. Do you need Shadow?"

"No, I need to be strong enough to face this." She squeezed his arm before pulling away. "I want to do whatever I can to help those children."

"I think you've been amazing with them tonight."

She chuckled. "I was trying to remember all the books I read when I was pregnant. They're probably out of date now. Ultimately, though, I'm winging it. I confess, too, that I'm drawing on some of my experience as a dog trainer. Gentle when I can be, firm when I need to be. I want them to know I'm the boss, but I care, and I'll be fair with them. Mostly, I'm crossing my fingers and praying I don't screw anything up."

"Well, it seems to be working."

She wrapped her fingers around her mug to keep them warm. "I know you have to call Family Services and KCPD, but can't we at least wait until morning? They've had a hard three days and Abby still has a slight fever. They need their rest."

"I'm not calling Family Services."

"You're not turning them over to their father, are you? He can't take care of himself, much less two children."

Garrett set down his mug, snagged her hand, and pulled her out into the living room. "I have to call my contact at KCPD to let them know the children have been found. But we won't notify the father yet. There are some things you and I need to discuss."

"I bet. Did you see the bruise on Nate's face? Someone hit him."

"I saw." Garrett halted, his hand suddenly tight around hers. "What about Abby?"

"I didn't see any marks on her," she reassured him. "As protective as he is of her, I can see Nate standing between her and any kind of threat. But they're both suffering from neglect. Their clothes don't fit. They aren't being fed. I'd like to do some shopping for them tomorrow." She tugged him along behind her and sat on the sofa. "Do you know who the bald man is Nate talked about?"

"I think so." Garrett settled onto the cushion beside her and pulled up another picture on his phone. This one was a mugshot of a beefy, brutal-looking man with bushy dark eyebrows and a shaved head. To cap off his arrogant, intimidating look, he had a black skull tattooed on either side of his scalp. "This is Kai Olivera. He's the reason you and the children are staying hidden here tonight instead of going back to KC. He's bad news. Drugs. Human trafficking. Illegal arms sales. He started off as a gangbanger and worked his way up to being king of his own criminal empire."

"I think I'm scared of him, too." She shuddered and

looked away from the image. "How would Nate and Abby meet someone like him?" When Garrett hesitated, she pushed. "You need to tell me everything. If they're staying here and we have to protect them, I need to know what we're up against."

His rugged face softened with a smile that didn't quite reach his eyes. "I like how you say 'we.' That you see us as a team."

"You aren't going to leave us here alone, in case one of these guys shows up, are you?"

"No."

"Then, yes, we're a team."

His shoulders lifted with a deep breath, and then he got down to the business of explaining just what kind of threat Nate and Abby were facing. "Swiegert works for Olivera. Started off as a customer, now he helps him move product."

"Product? Their dad's a drug dealer, too?"

He nodded. "And he's still using, based on what I saw this afternoon. I don't know if Zane Swiegert sent his kids away to protect them from Olivera, or if they figured out for themselves that they were in a dangerous situation. I need to talk to them ASAP and find out what they know."

"They need their sleep first," Jessica insisted. "And another good meal."

"Agreed. I'm going to hang around and keep an eye on the place tonight. I'd like to talk to Nate in the morning after breakfast." He angled himself toward her, then pulled her hands between his, chuffing them to warm them up. "I'm also going to introduce you to the detective who's running the KCPD task force to bring down Olivera. Conor Wildman. He and his team will help us protect the kids, but I want you to be familiar with their faces. You see anyone around here you don't know, you lock yourself and the kids in the house, and you call me or Conor."

"I will. I was thinking of installing some more security cameras, too."

"You're a woman after my own heart."

She turned her hands to still his massage and let them settle atop his thigh. "I thought the way to a man's heart was through his stomach," she teased.

"Not mine. I've been at this too long and have seen too much. Knowing the things I care about are well guarded and secure? That's what makes me happy." He grinned. "Although I wouldn't turn my nose up at a homemade pie."

"Duly noted." Jessica looked toward the kitchen. "I think I still have a bag of cherries I pitted and froze last summer after picking them off of Gran's trees out back."

"Wait. You bake?" He sank into the back of the sofa and raked his fingers through his hair. "Ah, hell. How am I ever going to keep my hands off you now?"

She laughed out loud at that, appreciating that they could lighten the mood between them after sharing such a heavy discussion about druggies and dealers and task forces that were all interested in the two children sleeping upstairs.

But this was a serious discussion, and she'd asked to know everything Garrett did. "So, what happens now? How long can the children stay with me? And are we far enough away from Kansas City that there's not an imminent threat from Kai Olivera or their father?"

"Let me make my phone calls." Garrett pushed to his feet and headed for the hall tree to retrieve his hat. "Sit tight for tonight. I'll be back to interview Nate in the morning."

"You're not staying the night?" After that talk about security protocols and safeguarding things he cared about, she was surprised that he was leaving.

"Not that I didn't enjoy wearing you like a blanket last night…" Her face heated at the memory of just how needy she'd been. "But it's probably for the best, so the kids don't stumble in and find a man they only met a couple of hours ago asleep in your bed. I'd rather they build trust in you, so they have at least one adult they'll turn to before they decide running away again is their best option, rather than have me scare them off. Abby didn't say a word to me, so she might be afraid of men. Nate? He's still sizing me up. I'm not sure if he trusts the badge or not. I'm guessing he expected a cop to help them somewhere along the way, and they let him down. I'll be fine in my truck."

His reasoning made sense. Although, she believed if Nate and Abby got to know him, they'd learn he was another adult they could trust. "You don't think that will look suspicious that you're sleeping in your truck if anyone is watching the place? What if you stay in one of the other guest rooms? Or on the couch?"

He considered her invitation for a moment, then hooked his ball cap back on the hall tree, a sure sign he was staying. "The couch. That will put me between the door and you three upstairs." She nodded, feeling relieved to know he'd be there with them. "I've already called in one of my officers to keep an eye on the outside tonight. Plainclothes. I don't want to draw any attention to your place in case Swiegert or Olivera or someone else who works for him is looking for the kids out this way. Since I'm a regular visitor, my departmental truck shouldn't look too out of place."

"Should I cancel my training sessions tomorrow?" she asked. "Call Hugo and Soren and tell them to stay away?"

Garrett shook his head. "I think you should keep your routine as normal as possible. The neighbors will talk if you start making calls like that. Olivera is going to have his people out trying to find information on those kids. An abrupt change in routine or building this place up like a fortress will get the gossips' tongues wagging, That's the kind of intel Olivera will want to check out."

"Will we be safe with just you and your friend Conor? You know I don't keep any guns in the house. After John…"

"I understand. With the kids here, I don't want them to have access to firearms, either. I'll keep my rifle locked in my truck, but I'd like to keep my sidearm with me. Conor will be armed, too."

She nodded. "You had your gun last night, and I was mostly okay with it."

Garrett reached out and caught a loose tendril of her hair. He rubbed it between his thumb and fingers before tucking it behind her ear. He feathered his fingers into the hair at her nape and cupped the side of her neck and jaw. "I'm sorry I can't do better than *mostly okay*. But I'm not going to leave you or Nate and Abby unprotected."

"I know you won't. But it's not all on your shoulders, Garrett." She looked toward the front door. "A dozen dogs on the property, remember? We'll know someone's here long before they get to the house."

"You're sure about me staying here? I would like to be close by."

"I'm sure." She wrapped her fingers around his wrist and tilted her cheek into his touch. "I'll bring down a pillow and some blankets for you."

He nodded his thanks. "Why don't you go on up to bed. I'll get my go-bag from my truck so I can change out of my uniform, then I'll lock everything up behind me. Keep Shadow upstairs with you. He'll sound the alarm if anything gets past me."

She didn't like the sound of that. "Don't get dead protecting us, okay? I wouldn't deal very well with that."

"I won't. Good night, Jessie."

She stood there, still holding on to his wrist, not moving away. "Aren't you going to kiss me goodnight?" She wasn't sure if she sounded seductive or pathetic. It had been a long time since she'd felt enough for a man that the difference mattered. "You said you were going to kiss me again."

"Maybe you should kiss me, instead," he teased. But his smile quickly faded, and he pulled away at her wide-eyed response to his dare. "Sorry. I said I wouldn't push."

"No, I…" She grabbed a handful of his shirt to keep him from retreating. She willed those handsome green eyes to understand that she was trying, but that none of this flirty, intimate banter came easily for her. "You understand I'm the queen of slow movers when it comes to relationships. It has been a long time since I even wanted to try. Not since John."

"Ah, honey. I don't know what to say to that. I've cared about you for so long. I want more, but I don't want to screw anything up."

Releasing the front of his shirt, she wound her arms around his waist and hugged him. She hated that his protective vest created a barrier between them, but she found the gap between the bottom of the vest and the top of his utility belt and clung to the warmth emanating from the man underneath. His strong arms folded around her, and she nestled her forehead against the base of his throat. "I'm just glad you're here. You're warm and strong and…you ground me. You keep me out of the dark places in my head and keep me moving forward. I'm used to handling everything on my own—well, with Shadow's help. But I feel stronger when you're with me—like, I can handle whatever I have to because you're here to back me up if I need it."

"Just like Shadow. I'm your support man."

She shifted her hold on him, leaning back against his arms and framing his rugged, wonderfully tactile face between her hands, then tipped his face down to hers. "Not like Shadow. I would never kiss him on the lips."

Feeling brave, Jessica pushed up on tiptoe and pressed a sweet kiss to his mouth. His response was infinitely patient, his lips resting pliantly as she explored his mouth and learned the different textures of his beard and lips and tongue. Then he captured her bottom lip between his, to taste, to suckle. The tips of her breasts grew hard and strained against the itchy lace of her bra. Her pulse thundered in her ears and the long-forgotten weight of molten desire pooled between her legs. There was no plunging, no claiming, just a tender exploration that went on and on until she frightened herself with how much more she wanted from this man.

When she pulled away with a stuttering breath and buried her head against his neck once more, Garrett tightened his arms around her. His lips pressed against her hair. "I could live on that kiss for days." His voice was a grumbly, deep-pitched whisper. "Thank you for pushing yourself out of your comfort zone."

"Thank you for being so patient with me."

"We'll get there." He pressed another kiss to her hair and closed his hands around her shoulders and pushed her away to arm's length. "I'm beat. I need to get some sleep, too. Go on." He turned her toward the stairs and playfully swatted her butt.

She whipped around, surprised by the touch.

"Too much?"

With a blush warming her face, she smiled. "My forty-six-year-old body appreciates that you like a little of what you see."

He leaned in, bracing his hands on the wall on either side of her and practically growled. "I like a lot of what I see. I liked a lot of what I felt smushed against me last night, too."

Resting her hand at the center of his chest, she tilted her eyes to his. "The feeling is mutual."

He pushed ever so gently against her hand, moving in as if he was going to kiss her again. But at the last moment, he turned his head, shoving his fingers through his rumpled hair and backing away. "Slow mover. I can respect that. It may drive me crazy, but you are totally worth the wait." He reached behind her to capture her braid and pulled it over her shoulder. He dragged his fingers along its entire length before resting it atop the swell of her breast. "I want you all-in with this relationship when it happens."

"*If* it happens."

He shook his head. "*When.* Tomorrow. A week from now. Two years down the road. You and me? We're gonna happen."

She shivered at the certainty of his promise. "Good night, Garrett. I'll see you in the morning."

She hurried up the steps to the linen closet to retrieve a pillow and cover for him. From the bottom of the stairs she heard, *"When."*

Chapter Eight

Garrett ignored the twinge in his back from sleeping on Jessie's couch and poured his second cup of coffee, biding his time until Nate polished off his stack of silver dollar pancakes, scrambled eggs, and bacon at the kitchen counter. It was a perfectly good couch. It was almost long enough for his body, and he'd been plenty warm. But he'd been half on alert against any noises inside or outside the house; he'd been half-hard after that incredibly sweet, mind-blowing kiss Jessie had initiated; he had a fifty-year-old back, and it was the couch.

Sleep seemed to be in short supply hanging around Jessie and K-9 Ranch, but he wouldn't trade his time here for anything in the world. This feeling of chaotic domestic bliss, this sense of home, had eluded him his entire adult life. But this morning, being a part of Jessie's world, he felt like this was where he belonged. This was what his life was supposed to be like. Although he wore his gun and badge on his belt, he was dressed down in jeans and a navy-blue T-shirt, enjoying what was, for him, a leisurely morning. And a twinge of back pain wasn't going to dampen the pleasure of sharing this morning with Jessie, Nate, and Abby one little bit.

He leaned his hips against the counter and watched Jessie help Abby up onto a stepstool beside her to show the little girl how to make pancakes on the griddle pan. Jessie had carefully braided Abby's hair back into a pigtail that matched her own. And she was being very careful about keeping little fingers away from the hot griddle and the stove's gas burners. Garrett enjoyed the view on so many levels, watching the females work side by side. Jessie's backside in a pair of worn jeans was a thing of beauty. He had yet to hear the little girl speak to anyone except her brother, but she enthusiastically emulated Jessie and drank in everything she wanted to teach her. Abby was a beautiful child, sweet and delicate—but he suspected there was a lot of tomboy and modern woman inside her wanting to get out. He couldn't think of a better role model than Jessie Bennington, who'd overcome adversity, launched her second career, and made a living rescuing and helping dogs, children, clients in need, and even the occasional lonely workaholic deputy.

Even Toby and Shadow were circling the deck outside the French doors that led out back, leaving nose prints on the glass. He couldn't blame them for wanting to be a part of breakfast at Jessie's house, too.

He'd already gotten up to meet Hugo out in the barn to help with the dogs, goats, and morning chores—and to fill him in on the situation inside the house. Not that he expected the older man with a hearing aid and arthritic fingers to put himself in the line of fire should anything go down here at the ranch. But another set of eyes keeping watch on things and reporting anything unusual couldn't hurt. He intended to have a similar conversation with Hugo's grandson when he showed up for work this evening.

"Can I have more milk?" Nate slapped his empty glass down on top of the island.

"*May* I have more milk?" Jessie corrected without missing a beat. She turned and smiled at the boy. "And a *please* would be nice at the end of that sentence."

Nate rolled his eyes and huffed out an annoyed breath. But he did what was asked of him. "May I have more milk, please?"

Garrett set his mug down and reached for the glass. "I've got it." He opened the fridge and refilled the glass, then set it on the counter. "And now you would say…?"

Nate's blue eyes met his. "Thanks."

"You're welcome." He nodded over his shoulder toward the woman at the stove. "And who made your breakfast?"

"Thanks, Jessie."

"Thank you, Jessie." Garrett added his own gratitude, showing Nate that he wasn't singling out the boy and asking him to do anything he wouldn't do himself. "Home cooking beats a microwaved burrito at the station house."

She turned and shared a pretty smile. "You're both welcome."

Nate didn't pick up the glass until Garrett released it completely. But then the boy drank half of it in a few big gulps. The milk mustache left behind on his top lip reminded Garrett that Nate Swiegert was still a little boy, despite his very grown-up efforts to protect his sister and get them both to safety.

Garrett checked his watch. Detective Wildman would be here soon, and then the busy normalcy of this morning would be erased by some serious police work and outlining the rules of protective custody for Nate and Abby.

"Are you sure we won't get into trouble if we don't go to school today?" Nate asked. He glanced at Garrett but directed the question to Jessie.

"Nope. Think of this like your spring break. Although, I did print off some math facts you can practice to keep your skills sharp. Plus, I want you to do some reading on your own. Then I'm going to give you another lesson on how to work with the dogs."

"Sweet." Nate was clearly excited about a chance to be with the dogs again.

Abby turned on her stool. "Natey, can I come look at the dogs with you?"

Jessie answered. "I want you to take it easy today, Miss Abby. Your fever may be gone this morning, but I don't want you to do too much and get sick again." She smoothed the little girl's braid behind her back, an affectionate gesture meant to ease the sting of denying her dog-time. "I want you to take a nap if you feel sleepy. Otherwise, I'd like you to show me all the letters and numbers you know how to write, and we'll practice writing your name." Jessie tapped the end of Abby's nose. "And if you're still feeling good this afternoon, we'll go out to the barn to visit Penny and her pups. I'm sure Charlie misses you."

Abby clapped her hands in little girl excitement. She glanced back at her brother, as if checking to see if her enthusiasm was warranted, and when he nodded, she beamed a smile up at Jessie.

Jessie smiled right back, looking as light and un-encumbered by the past as Garrett had ever seen her. "See all the holes in the pancake where the bubbles have popped?" Abby nodded. Jessie slipped the spatula into the girl's hand and curled her own fingers around it. "That means it's time to flip your pancakes. They're almost done."

Abby might not have spoken to anyone besides her brother, but that didn't mean she wasn't interacting with Jessie. Or Garrett. The little girl celebrated her first successful-ish pancake by scooping it onto the spatula and holding it out to him. Her smile was the best invitation Garrett could have. "Hey. You did a great job." When she continued to hold out the small, misshapen pancake, Garrett realized it was a gift. "Oh. You want me to eat it? You don't want to eat your first one?"

Apparently, eye-rolling ran in the family.

Garrett grinned and reached for the offering. "Thank you, Abby." The pancake was freshly made, and still hot to the touch, but he picked it off the spatula, rolled it up and stuffed the whole thing into his mouth. "That's really yummy." He wasn't lying when he smiled and praised her. "Good job."

Her answering smile was worth the heat that singed the roof of his mouth.

Garrett poured himself some cold milk and drank it down. As he cooled his mouth, he looked over the rim of the glass and caught Nate watching his reaction to Abby's overture of friendship—possibly to make sure he didn't say or do anything that would upset his sister. Every choice Nate made, from running away to sleeping arrangements to keeping his eye on Garrett reaffirmed his suspicions that Nate was protecting Abby from something horrendous. His blood boiled with the possibilities of what that could mean and made him more anxious to interview Nate to get the answers he and the KCPD task force needed. And, it doubled his determination to keep this little family of circumstance safe from the evil that had chased them out of Kansas City.

Needing to keep his hands busy and his demeanor calm so he wouldn't become the thing that frightened these children, Garrett opened the dishwasher and started loading the dishes, glasses, and utensils they'd used. His movements must have been a little too sharp because when he straightened to rinse out the mixing bowl and whisk Jessie had used, he found her watching him over the top of Abby's head. The look of concern stamped on her face told him he wasn't fooling anybody with his just-another-morning-on-the-ranch routine.

"You okay?" She mouthed the words.

Garrett exhaled his anger on a heavy breath and raked his fingers through his hair. She turned off the stove and pushed the griddle to the back while he went back to the dishes.

A knock at the front door made him pause. "That'll be Conor." Garrett had already warned the children that an adult should always answer the door. But when Jessie automatically headed out of the kitchen, he grabbed her by the elbow and pulled her behind him. "Just in case it's not someone we know, let me go first."

She nodded, then reached up to straighten his short hair. The caring gesture eased some of the anger that was still scalding like acid through his veins. "Once I meet your friend, you can talk to Nate in the living room. I'll keep Abby busy in the kitchen or upstairs."

"Thanks."

"Of course. Remember, you're the adult, even though Nate plays like he is. Be gentle with him. He's a little boy who's been scared out of his mind, not a hardened criminal."

Garrett mimicked the same caress, gently brushing a loose strand of silvery-gold hair off her forehead. "I won't make things any worse, I promise."

WORSE FOR NATE, NO.

Worse for Garrett…?

He was vibrating with the kind of anger he hadn't felt since he'd seen a terrorist strap a bomb to his own child and send him out to greet the convoy of soldiers while Garrett and his spotter watched and provided cover from higher ground. He'd warned his team over their radios about the shifting makeup of the crowd. In a matter of seconds, the friendly greeting had morphed into an attack. With his teammates trapped among supposed friendlies who had suddenly become their enemy, Garrett had been forced to pick off the insurgents in the crowd targeting the soldiers—including the boy with the bomb—so that his team could rescue their wounded and escape.

With his hand clenched into a fist behind his back, he listened to Nate tell his story to Conor Wildman.

To Conor's credit, the detective kept the conversation going with a few calmly voiced questions. But Garrett could tell by the tight clench of the detective's jaw that the boy's story was getting to him, too.

"And that's the night when the bald man and his friends hurt your father?" Conor asked.

Nate nodded. He'd already identified a picture of Kai Olivera as the *bald man*. He'd never actually been introduced to the drug dealer, so he didn't recognize his name, but called him by the apt descriptor. He'd forced his way into their apartment one night to have a *conversation* with his father. He'd also shared the creep's fascination with Abby after another visit where he'd held his sister on his lap the entire meeting.

"Dad didn't have his money." Because he'd been snorting the coke himself with his girlfriend du jour and had passed out instead of making deliveries and picking up payments from the dealers on his route. It was bad enough that Nate had witnessed his father getting high in their apartment and had had to make peanut butter and jelly sandwiches for dinner for himself and Abby. But the fact that he'd seen Olivera and two of his enforcers punishing Zane left a foul taste in Garrett's mouth. But Nate continued on matter-of-factly recounting his experience as if he was telling them about his day at school. "I hid Abby under her bed when they started fighting. I told her to stop crying and be as quiet as her doll, so no one knew she was there. But Dad stopped when they dropped the end of the sofa on his hand. My dad cried, too. Real men aren't supposed to cry."

"They do if they're hurting as much as I suspect your father was," Conor said, trying to show a little sympathy for a man who'd blown his responsibilities to his family in so many ways. Zane Swiegert was still Nate's father, and the boy probably had a lot of mixed feelings about the man. "Did you try to help him?"

Nate nodded, his gaze darting from Conor to Garrett and back. "The bald man knocked me down. He called me a little baby and said I was in the way. He told me to go back to my room and let the men settle things."

Settling things between Kai Olivera and Zane was when the most heinous bargain of all had been made.

Olivera would cancel Zane's debt and let him live in exchange for Abby.

Garrett's nails cut crescent-shaped divots in the palm of his hand as he replayed those words over and over in his head. A sweet little girl as payment for a drug debt?

No wonder Zane Swiegert was so desperate to find his children. But was he trying to save them? Or his own skin? Either way, Kai Olivera wasn't putting another hand on Nate, and he wasn't taking Abby.

No. Never. Not gonna happen.

Not while there was still breath in Garrett's body.

He could see that Conor was having trouble dealing with the information Nate was sharing, too. He paused long enough that Nate squirmed uncomfortably in his chair. The detective held up a hand, asking Nate to be patient a few minutes longer. Conor's nostrils flared with a deep breath. "You're certain that's what the bald man said? He'd let your father live if he *gave* him your sister?"

"I locked the door to our bedroom, and I laid down on the floor. I could hear the men talking through the gap underneath my door."

"And your dad agreed to the deal?" Conor asked.

For the first time, Nate hesitated to answer. "Abby was scared. She didn't want to go with the bald man. He said he'd give Dad twenty-four hours to pay him back, one way or the other."

"Did your dad help you run away? Or did he agree to the deal?"

For the first time, Garrett saw a sheen of tears in Nate's blue eyes. But the moment he remembered his assertion that crying was a weakness, he angrily swiped the tears away. "Dad said we could never be a family again, that he didn't want us anymore. He said I had to take Abby away and keep her safe. He gave me twenty dollars he'd stashed in the freezer and said we weren't ever to come home again."

Conor closed his notebook and tucked it back inside the pocket of his suit jacket. "He gave you the responsibility of being the parent instead of doing the job himself?"

Nate's legs swung like pistons beneath his chair. He clearly was done sitting still and answering questions. "I want to go check on Abby. Okay?"

Garrett never wanted to hug a child as badly as he wanted to hold Nate. But that wasn't what Nate needed right now. In addition to some serious professional counseling, what this brave boy needed right now was contact with the one family member he could rely on. He needed to know that his sacrifice to protect his sister hadn't been in vain. Learning to trust another adult would come with time. He hoped.

Garrett stood abruptly, ending the interview, allowing all three of them to catch their breaths and ease some of the tension from the room. "Thank you for talking to us, Nate. You've helped a lot. We'll be able to find the men who hurt you and your dad, and the information will help us do a better job of keeping you and Abby safe." He laid his hand on Nate's shoulder, and though the nine-year-old didn't jerk away, he didn't exactly warm to Garrett's touch, either. "Although, you might have to tell your story again someday."

"To a judge?"

Garrett nodded.

"Will you help my dad, too?"

Not high on his list of priorities, but it was important to Nate. Garrett squeezed his shoulder before releasing him. "You and your sister are my first priority. But if I can do anything for your dad, I'll try. You understand that he's broken the law? That if I see him, I'll have to arrest him?"

Nate nodded. "But the bald man will kill him if he can't find Abby."

Also true. "Yeah, bud." Garrett hooked his thumbs into his belt beside his gun and badge. "Between you, me, Jessie and Detective Wildman, we'll keep Abby safe." He glanced back to see that Conor was standing, too. "If Detective Wildman will help me, we'll do what we can to protect your dad, too."

"You bet." Conor pulled back the front of his jacket

and tucked his hands into the pockets of his slacks. "Thank you for your help this morning."

Nate considered the grown men's response to his request, no doubt weighing his conflicted loyalty to his father who'd created this dangerous situation against his desire to simply be a normal kid without life-or-death concerns.

Garrett tried to give him some of the latter. "You did good, Nate. Abby and Jessie are on the back deck. If you want, you can go out with them and play with Toby. But stay where we can see you. I need to talk to Detective Wildman for a few minutes."

He ran all the way through the house to the back door before he stopped and turned. "You're not gonna ask Abby any of these questions, are you?" Even drawn up to his full height, Nate stood two feet shorter than Garrett, but he heard the man-to-man tone in the boy's voice. "She won't talk to you. Talking about the bald man makes her cry."

"You aren't the only one protecting her now, Nate. I'll do everything in my power to keep you and your sister safe."

Nate evaluated Garrett's promise, shrugged, then pulled open the back door. "Okay." He charged across the deck to the railing overlooking the back yard. "Toby!"

The black Lab loped up the steps to accept the bacon the boy had stashed in his pocket. Then the two were chasing and wrestling across the back deck.

Conor stepped up beside Garrett. "If he's this good a witness in a courtroom deposition, Kai Olivera will go away forever."

"If Nate makes it to a courtroom." Garrett glanced at the younger man and shook his head. "This isn't just about your damn task force. He's nine years old, for God's sake. He shouldn't have to testify. He shouldn't even know about drugs and enforcers and protecting his sister from a deviant like Olivera."

"You think Olivera wants to sell her or keep her?"

"Does it matter?" Garrett shoved his fingers through his hair. He'd kept his cool for about as long as he could manage. "He doesn't get to touch her again. Ever."

"Agreed. One hundred percent. But it could decide whether I cut off his head or his private parts when I arrest him." Right. He'd forgotten that Wildman used wicked sarcasm to dispel the tension he felt.

Garrett needed something more physical. He started pacing. "That's why he waited so long to report them missing. He was giving them a head start."

"And now Olivera is probably putting the screws to him pretty hard to find his payment for the missing drugs and money."

Garrett eyed the younger man. "You need someone from your task force to pick up Swiegert and put him in protective custody."

"It's on my to-do list. But Swiegert's gone to ground since our interview yesterday. He probably realized how much trouble he's in."

"Or he's somewhere getting high again. Drowning his sorrows. Easing his pain. Forgetting he even has kids."

Conor pulled out his phone to check his messages.

"There's nothing new from any of my team. You don't think Olivera took him out already, do you?"

Garrett paced across the living room. "What's it going to do to those children if he gets killed?"

"My question is, why wouldn't he take the children and run away with them?"

He paced back to the kitchen. "An addict with only twenty dollars, a broken hand, and a lowlife like Olivera after him is a lot harder to hide than two small children."

"Take my pocket change and run?" Conor shook his head. "It's not much of a plan."

"He's not much of a father."

"Sounds like you've gotten pretty attached to those kids already," the detective speculated.

"They're important to Jessie, and that makes them important to me." He raked his fingers through his hair. That wasn't the whole truth. "Kids in danger is a real trigger for me. Goes back to my time in the Army. Innocent bystanders getting killed? Children brainwashed by a parent or elder to sacrifice themselves for the cause? I just want them to be safe and not have to worry about the kind of crap you and I take care of every day."

Conor's grim expression indicated he understood where he was coming from.

Conor punched in a number on his phone and put it up to his ear. "I'll see if I can call in reinforcements to help track down Swiegert."

"What if he's complicit in all this?" Garrett felt his blood pressure rising. "What if Swiegert doesn't give a damn about those kids, and he wants to find Abby and make the payment as badly as Olivera does? Use his daughter to get back in his boss's good graces?"

He stopped midstride and braced his hands at his waist and stared out the back door windows. Jessie was working with a small terrier mix and showing Abby the hand signals to get the dog to sit and stay. Although Abby was more about rewarding the dog with treats and exchanging pets for licks than in learning the actual skills, she was talking—to the dog. Nate had found a Frisbee and sent it flying from the edge of the deck. Toby was off like a big black bullet, chasing it down and leaping at the last moment to catch the disk squarely in his mouth. Then Jessie showed him how to call the dog to return to him. Nate's narrow shoulders puffed up when the Lab did exactly as he asked, trotting up the stairs and dropping the disk at his feet for a reward of more petting and a treat. Nate threw the disk again and Toby was off to the races.

It was a normal scene. They were having fun. They were being kids.

The inside of Garrett's stomach burned with the goodness of it all, and just how quickly these moments of happiness could be destroyed.

He sensed the distant contact and shifted his gaze to find Jessie staring back at him, frowning with questions and concern.

Garrett blinked and quickly turned away. He ran into Conor Wildman's watchful blue eyes. "You okay?" the detective asked.

"I need a minute." He didn't bother trying to gloss

over his dark mood. The detective was too perceptive for that. He heard Abby squeal in delight and Jessie laughing through the back door behind him. He was jealous that they could find any happiness in all of this. And he didn't intend to spoil that for them. He pointed a commanding finger at the detective. "You got eyes on them for now?"

"I got this." He nodded toward the front door. "Go. Burn off your steam. I need you to have your head in the game. I don't want to traumatize these kids any more than you do."

Garrett slammed the door behind him and hurried down the porch steps. His first thought was to get in his truck and drive fast to somewhere, anywhere. But the rational voice in his head reminded him that he was the protection detail. He might not be a sniper staking down a rooftop or a mountain ridge. But he was the backup he'd promised KCPD he'd provide. He was the last line of defense who would keep Jessie, Nate, and Abby, and this whole damn county safe from Swiegert, Olivera, and his crew. He wouldn't abandon his post.

He stalked past his truck and headed to the barn. The dogs raised a cacophony of alert and excited barks as he passed their kennels. Rex came around the side of the barn, identified him, then loped away to whatever corner of the property he was patrolling today.

The cooler air of the barn tempered his anger for a moment. But then the images of everything Nate had told him filled his head. He hadn't been there, but he'd fought in a war, he'd worked a SWAT team, he'd led his patrol division to every kind of call imaginable. His imagination was as vividly clear as if he'd witnessed all Nate Swiegert had for himself.

An overmuscled, tattooed thug cradling sweet, quiet Abby on his lap and not giving a damn that the little girl was crying.

Nate finding his dad passed out on the living room floor and dragging the grown man's body over to the couch.

A nine-year-old boy wearing clothes that no longer fit him staring into empty kitchen cabinets and finally making a dinner of peanut butter and jelly sandwiches for him and his five-year-old sister. Again.

A desperate, broken man sending his young children out into the world with a twenty-dollar bill, as if that alone would protect them from the evils pursuing them.

Kai Olivera smiling with a devilish expression that matched the skulls on his temples telling Zane Swiegert he could pay his debt with his little girl.

With a feral roar, Garrett swung around and punched his fist against the post beside one of the stalls.

He heard Mama Penny's yelp of surprise a second before he felt the hands closing over his forearm and pulling his arm down to his side.

"Garrett." Jessie's firm voice called him from the depths of his mind. Every muscle in his forearm was tense beneath her grip. "You're bleeding." Then one hand was cupping the side of his jaw and angling his face down to hers. He was drowning in the turbulent gray waters of her beautiful eyes tilted up to his. "You keep it together, Garrett Caldwell. Those kids don't need anyone else scaring them."

He breathed in deeply, once, twice, willing the anger to leave him. But it only morphed into a sense of help-lessness. "Are they safe?"

"Yes. I left them with Detective Wildman and Shadow. You're the one I'm worried about. I could see you were upset. When you stormed out of the house—"

Upset? Hell yeah, he was upset. There were so many good people in this world who'd been denied children. Like this woman right here. Like Hayley. Like him. While Zane Swiegert had those two brave, beautiful children to call his own. His hand curled into a fist again. "Who does that? It's bad enough that he forced that boy to be the adult in the family. That he let Oli-vera hit him. But he'll leave him alone if he hands Abby over to him? Who sells his own child?"

"A monster. Not a man." Her steady voice calmed him. He focused on where she touched him—his face, his forearm. He couldn't even feel the pain where the skin over his knuckles had split. "What those children need right now is a good man. Nate, especially, needs to talk to and spend time with someone who shows him how a real man acts. That's you, Garrett. He needs *you*."

But all he could see was that little Afghan boy again, his father guilting him or brainwashing him or tricking him into sacrificing himself to take out a few American soldiers. The memory of how he'd had to line him up in the crosshairs of his rifle scope and pull the trigger before the boy could detonate the bomb was as vivid as the bruise on Nate's face. Using a child. Throwing away a child. "Zane Swiegert doesn't deserve to be a father."

"Maybe not. But you can't think about that right now. You have to think about the children. You have to let go of your anger and focus on what they need."

"What about what I need? What about what you need?"

"What do you mean—?"

Garrett captured Jessie's sweet face between his hands and crashed his mouth down over hers. Anger morphed into passion. Desire morphed into need. Her lips parted beneath his and he thrust his tongue inside to taste the essence of coffee and bacon and Jessie herself. When her arms came around his neck, he skimmed his hands down her back, pulling her body flush with his. But it wasn't enough. It wasn't nearly enough.

The frantic need he felt wasn't all one-sided, either, and Jessie's eagerness fueled his own. Her fingertips pawed at the nape of his neck. And then with a moan deep in her throat, she grabbed a fistful of his T-shirt in one hand while the other swept against the grain of his hair, exciting him with hundreds of tiny caresses before she palmed the back of his head and turned him to an angle that allowed her to nip at his chin, press a kiss to the corner of his mouth, then allow some mutual plundering of each other's lips again.

His blood caught fire, burning the anger from his system and leaving him aware of her lush mouth and womanly curves plastered against his harder angles. Needing more, wanting everything, he palmed her butt with both hands and lifted her into his heat. Her breasts flattened beneath his chest as he pushed her back against the post and trapped her there. He finally tore his mouth from hers and trailed his lips along her jaw until he captured her earlobe and pulled it between his teeth. She shivered against him and breathed his name.

He'd gone so long without this. So long without her. So long without love.

"Garrett." She wrapped one leg behind his knee, giving him the access to thrust himself helplessly against her heat. Her lips brushed against the throbbing pulse in his neck. "Garrett, we have to—" he claimed her mouth again and poured everything he was feeling in one last kiss "—need to stop."

"I know."

His body was going to hate him for this. But as her fingers eased their tight grip on his hair and neck, he pulled his mouth from hers, pressing one light kiss, then two, to her warm, swollen lips before he let her feet slide to the ground and he rested his forehead against hers. He was hard as a rock inside his jeans, not bad for a man his age, but he felt lighter, saner, more grounded now that he and Jessie had taken their fill of each other.

It took a little longer to even out his breathing. A few moments more before he could fully lose himself in the stormy gray eyes looking up at him.

"I'm sorry." He gently rubbed his hands up and down her arms. "I'm sorr—"

"Don't." Her fingers came up to sweep across his mouth, reminding him just how sensitized they were after that kiss on steroids. "Don't you dare apologize for losing it a little with me. After twelve years, I sometimes forget what passion feels like. How…heady it is to be needed like that."

"I didn't give you much choice."

"If I had said no, you would have stopped."

"You've got that much faith in me?"

"Yes. I know you have demons, too, Garrett. And the story Nate shared with you and Conor triggered them. But I also know you are a protector down to your core. If you weren't, you wouldn't have gotten so upset." She ran her hands across his chest and shoulders, as if smoothing out the wrinkles she might have left there. Then she leaned back and took a stab at straightening his hair. He treasured the gentle caresses as much as he did every kiss they shared. "Are you better?"

He was. He'd needed a physical outlet for his emotions, and she'd somehow known and been there for him. Such a strong woman, yet so caring and feminine. "Feeling a little raw," he confessed. "But better."

"Good." She pulled his hand from her arm and turned so she could put even more space between them. "Now let me see your injury."

She cradled his bigger hand gently between hers to inspect how his knuckles had fared against the post. She clicked her tongue, then grabbed his wrist and tugged him into step behind her.

She paused at the first storage room door, inserted a key into the lock, and opened it. Larger than the room that had been broken into, this one had a huge stainless steel sink where she could wash the dogs. She turned on the water and pulled his hand beneath the warm stream to clean the debris out of his wound while she opened a cabinet and pulled out a first aid kit and a bottle of hydrogen peroxide. She hooked her foot around a tall stool and pulled it out from beside the sink. "Have a seat."

He turned off the water and dutifully sat in front of her while she used a clean towel to dry his skin and gently dab at the blood seeping from his split knuckles. "Did I hear you correctly? Zane Swiegert plans to use Abby to pay off his debt to Olivera?"

Garrett nodded. "Nate overheard his dad talking to Olivera. That makes him a witness. Swiegert and Olivera are going to want to shut him up so he can't talk to the cops or testify against them."

"His own father?"

"Supposedly, it was his idea for the kids to run away, but…" Garrett swore under breath. "Drugs change a man. I'm sure Swiegert didn't mean to endanger his children, but a desperate man does desperate things. And the main thing an addict is thinking about is his next fix. Not his job, not his family, not even his own health. I think they're both a threat."

He raised an eyebrow at Jessie's answering curse. "I will not lose another child, Garrett. Not to the kind of violence you're talking about. I can't."

He stilled her hand beneath his. "We won't let that happen. Between KCPD and my team, we'll keep round-the-clock watch on your house." She nodded and went back to work. "And I'm moving in until this is over. *I* am going to watch over you and the kids. I want to talk escape strategies and survival protocol with you and them, too."

"I'm okay with that." She soaked a cotton ball with the disinfectant. "Do you want to talk about it?"

"When I think about what Olivera wants to do with Abby. How he hit and belittled Nate…it takes me back to some places I don't want to go." He winced at the sting of peroxide on his open wound. The foolish mistake of punching the barn post was certainly bringing him back to reality. "My wife dying wasn't the only reason I had to leave the Army. They could have put me behind a desk or in a training camp. But I couldn't guarantee that I could take the shot anymore."

"Those flashbacks are a bitch, right?" Although he was at first taken aback by the vehemence of her words, he looked up to see a smug smile on her face. She beat back her demons every damn day. He would do the same. "Want me to train a therapy dog for you?"

He chuckled. "Nah. I've got *you.*"

"I'm your therapy *woman*?"

He stopped her doctoring and reached up to tag her behind the neck to meet her eyes and make sure she understood just how serious he was about the two of them. "You said I ground you. That I'm the solid, reliable man you can depend on. I feel the same way about you. I've seen and lost too much in my life. But with you, all that becomes the past. You make me want to stay in the present and look forward, not back. I see what the future looks like when I'm with you. I see everything that's missing in my life. I want that future. I like how I feel when I'm with you. Please give me the chance to love you, Jessie. I feel like you're the reward for surviving everything I've lost."

She shook her head with a wry smile and concentrated on wrapping the self-stick tape to keep the gauze in place around his hand. "I've got too many hang-ups to be anybody's reward."

"I don't want perfect. I want perfect for me." He touched two fingers to the point of her chin and tilted her face up to his. "That's you. I want you. I need you."

"Garrett…"

"I know, I know. I'm too intense and you're a slow mover. Let's get through this mess with Olivera and Swiegert first. Make sure those children are safe and in a loving home. Then maybe I can woo you at your pace." He released her when he could feel the apprehension vibrating through her. "This may feel sudden to you, but it's not to me. I love you, Jessie Bennington. I know it in every bone of my body. I just hope that one day you'll take a chance on loving me, too."

"I want that, too, Garrett." *But…* That unspoken word echoed through the small room. She turned away to drop the soiled items into the trash. "I don't know if I can convey just how scared…"

Her voice trailed away when his phone buzzed in his pocket. As a lawman, he couldn't ignore a potential emergency. He read the number. "It's Conor." He rose to his feet. "Caldwell here."

"You need to get in here." It wasn't the five-alarm emergency of intruders on the premises, but it was an emergency nonetheless. "There's something wrong with Ms. Bennington's dog. The kids are freaking out."

Garrett hung up and grabbed Jessie's hand in his injured one. "It's Shadow. He's having a seizure."

Chapter Nine

Jessica stood in the shadows of her living room watching Garrett stretched across her couch in a T-shirt and sweatpants. His bandaged hand was thrown up and resting on the pillow above his head. He'd kicked off the blanket and his feet were propped on the armrest. She wondered if he really could compartmentalize the stress and responsibility he took so seriously and relax his mind enough to sleep. Of course, he'd been burning the candle at both ends so much recently that maybe his body was exhausted enough that it wasn't giving him any choice but to sleep.

Hugging her arms around her waist, she leaned against the archway near the foot of the stairs and studied him from the top of his mussed salt-and-pepper hair down to the masculine length of his toes. Maybe this was enough, simply reassuring herself that he was here. Knowing he could be right beside her in a heartbeat if she needed him.

She admired the flat of his stomach and the narrow vertical strip of dark hair exposed between the hem of his shirt and the waistband of his pants. Even that was sprinkled with shards of silver hair, and she was curious to discover if all the hair on his chest was peppered like a silver fox. She'd loved John dearly, but it had been a long time since she'd felt so viscerally attracted to another man. She might not have all the lady parts she'd once had, but there were still other parts of her that stirred with unmistakable interest in all the things that made Garrett so distinctly male. Beard stubble. Firm lips. Deep voice. Broad shoulders. Muscled chest.

She was visually making her way down his sturdy thighs when one green eye blinked open.

"Jessie? You okay?"

She swung her gaze back up to his. "I can't sleep."

Both eyes were watching her now. "The kids?"

"Dead to the world."

"Shadow?"

"Fine. He responded to the pill as quickly as Hazel said he would and has been taking it easy ever since. I fear his loyalty has switched to Nate." She sighed, feeling both a little lost and happy she'd trained Shadow so well. "That dog is intuitive. He probably senses that Nate needs some unconditional love and support from a furry friend right now."

He held out his hand. "Do you want to cuddle?"

"Not exactly."

He swung his legs over the front of the sofa and sat up, looking wide-awake and a little worried now. "Talk to me."

Jessica straightened and crossed the room on silent feet. "I've been thinking about something you said today. In the barn."

"You mean when I was losing my—"

"No. After that."

"I'm sure it was pithy and life altering. What did I say?"

"You said I was your reward for surviving everything you've lost." She circled the coffee table and sat—close enough to feel his heat, but not close enough to touch. "I feel the same way. You're my reward for surviving. I'm so grateful you're part of my life. I'm grateful you're here with us now." She ducked her head, letting her loose waves fall around her face. She was uncertain until that very moment what she wanted to say to him. She tucked her hair behind her ears and raised her gaze to his again. "But I don't want gratitude to be the only thing between us."

"It's not."

"My *pace* is all about self-protection. I want to be braver than that. I want to live like you do. I want to love again. I'm falling in love with those children. And you know how I am with my dogs." He nodded, listening carefully, just one more thing that made it easy to open up to him. "You taking care of the things that are precious to me makes it awfully hard not to fall in love with you."

He reached over and tucked a wayward tendril of hair behind her ear. "I'm not doing it to impress you. Those things matter to me, too, because you matter." He arched an eyebrow. "But I am making progress with you?"

Very definitely. She stood, holding out her hand in invitation. "Come to bed with me."

"I'm comfortable with sleeping down here."

"I'm not."

Nodding his understanding of her sincerity, he pulled his gun and holster from the drawer of her coffee table and stood. Once he'd pocketed his phone, he took her hand and followed her up the stairs.

They paused to look in on the children and dog. All safe. All fast asleep.

"Is Conor or one of his men outside?" Jessica whispered.

Garrett pulled the door to, leaving an opening just wide enough for Shadow to step out if he needed to. "One of my officers, Levi Fox, is parked at the end of your driveway until his shift ends in the morning. Maya Hernandez will replace him until KCPD sends one of their unmarked cars out to take over."

She probably should be embarrassed by the state of her rumpled bed. But she'd tossed and turned, rethinking everything that had happened over the past few days and remembering the only time she'd truly relaxed was when Garrett had held her that first night here. Releasing his hand, she quickly straightened and fluffed the sheet and quilt, then sat on the edge of the bed and patted the mattress beside her. "I'm pretty rusty at this, but I want you."

He tucked his gun in the bedside table and set his phone on top. "To sleep? To hold you? Or something more?"

"Yes. All of that." Could she sound any more inexperienced, like she'd forgotten every sexual encounter she'd had? "Maybe in reverse order?"

He chuckled, and she tumbled into him as he sat on

the mattress beside her. He draped his arm around her shoulders and tangled his fingers in her long hair. The man was a furnace, and she instantly felt better being held against him. "Just to be clear, we're talking about making love? Then cuddling in the happy afterglow and falling asleep?"

Jessica pulled her knees up and let them fall over his thighs as she turned to wrap her arms around his waist. "Sounds like heaven to me. If you're up for it."

"Trust me. Around you, I always seem to be up for it." He pressed a kiss to the crown of her hair. "I just want you to be sure."

She laughed and remembered how much she loved a man who could make her laugh. Jessica cupped the side of his jaw, tickling her palm against the stubble of his beard, and angled his mouth down as she stretched up to meet him. "Let's start with a kiss. We can start where we were last night and end up where we were in the barn this afternoon."

"Sounds like a plan." He laughed as he closed the distance between them and covered her mouth in a gentle kiss.

Then he fell back across the bed, dragging her with him until she was lying on top of him. Just as she'd requested, the tender embrace soon became needy grabs and tongues melding together. Her thighs fell open on either side of his hips, giving her a clear indication that he was as into this mutual exploration as she was. His hands swept down her body, then back up, taking her shirt with it. He squeezed her bottom and pulled her up along his body until he latched on to the breast dangling above his mouth. He laved the tip with his tongue as he plumped the other in his hand.

Jessica groaned at the stinging heat that tightened her nipples into stiff beads and shot straight down between her legs. By the time he was done feasting on her other breast, she had pushed his shirt out of the way and found his own turgid male nipple to tease to attention among the crisp curls of silver and sable hair that dusted his chest. Her hair cascaded around their busy mouths and hands as she leaned over him, and it seemed to drive Garrett's urgency. He alternately tangled his fingers in the long, silky strands, murmuring words like, "Silky…soft…beauty…" before tugging just hard enough to bring her mouth back to his.

Then his arms banded around her, and he flipped them so that he was on top. He brushed her hair out in a halo around her head as she pushed his sweatpants down over his hips to reveal the erection she'd felt pressing against her. "Garrett…please."

In the next few seconds, her sleep shorts were gone and he was naked, kissing his way from her mouth down over her belly. It was her only moment of hesitation, and she grabbed his chin and turned his face up to hers. "I have scars," she gasped, her words breathy and uneven with desire for this man.

Garrett pushed himself up over her and dipped his head to reclaim her lips in a tender kiss. "So do I. Want to see them?"

"Not right now. Not really." She valiantly tried to remind him that she was forty-six, had been pregnant once, and bore the scars of both the bullet and her surgeries.

But he wasn't having any second thoughts. "Me, neither." He splayed his hand over her belly, touching it as if it was precious to him. "I mean, I care about what they mean. I care so much about you." He planted a quick kiss to her lips, then resumed his path down her body. "But seriously, Jessie. I'm a man. I've got it bad for you. And if I don't get inside you in the next few minutes, I'm going to embarrass myself and finish this off without you." His hand slid down to cup her, and she bucked against his grip. "Every inch of you is beautiful to me. Please. Let me do this."

All she could do was nod. And when he asked about protection, she kissed him again, thanking him for treating her like a normal, desirable woman. "I can't get pregnant, remember? And I haven't had sex since John died, so I'm clean."

"Me, too. Thank you for this gift."

"Thank you for making me feel safe enough to want this." He settled his hips over hers, nudging at her entrance, and the pressure building inside felt as exciting as it was unfamiliar. She wasn't some born-again spinster who'd gone too long since she'd been with a man. She understood now that she'd just been waiting for the one she wanted to be with. "Now, Garrett."

There was a little discomfort when he first pushed inside her. But with his thumb strumming her back to that wild readiness, they quickly fell into a timeless rhythm that neither age nor abstinence nor tragedy could ever completely erase. Jessica wound her legs around his hips and welcomed him with the sense that she was finally where she wanted to be. There were no acrobatics or fancy words, just a man and a woman and the love that had grown slowly and perfectly between them, finally reaching the light and blossoming into a feeling so right, she gasped with the pleasure of it.

She shattered into a million pieces and rode the shock waves as Garrett groaned with satisfaction and completed himself inside her.

Several minutes later, after bringing her a warm washcloth to clean and soothe her tender flesh, Garrett lay back and pulled her into his arms. She draped herself against him, deciding this closeness was much more enjoyable with no clothes between them. "Feeling okay, hon?"

Jessica would have laughed if she had the energy. She murmured, "Uh-hmm. You?"

"If I was any more okay, I'd be dead."

She was drifting off to a contented sleep as he covered them both and set the alarm on his phone. "I'll sneak out later before the kids wake in the morning. You can put a T-shirt back on then, too."

She kissed his chest, thanking him for his consideration. Then he closed his eyes. Embracing the knowledge that this was what happiness felt like, Jessica snuggled in and fell asleep.

SPENDING FIVE DAYS with Nate and Abby, and five nights with Garrett in her bed—not always making love, but always holding each other close—made Jessica feel like a young woman with a good life ahead of her again.

She was a little sore, a little tired, a little scared. But her life was filled with so much purpose now. She had more to look forward to than work. She basically homeschooled the children in the morning while Garrett went to work so that no one watching the house would think anything unusual about a sudden change in his schedule, while another officer either from the sheriff's office or KCPD watched over the house. She scheduled training sessions in the afternoon for her clients, while the children stayed indoors and out of sight.

And though she hadn't said the *love* word out loud, she felt it ready to burst from her heart. She felt it from Garrett, too. With each chaste kiss, every laugh, every smile. She felt it in the eager way he touched her body, and in the firm yet patiently paternal way he worked with Nate and Abby.

They had finally reported Nate and Abby being found to Family Services and, under strict orders from a judge, promised to keep their whereabouts secret until the danger had passed. The social worker who'd driven out to check on the welfare of the children had even agreed to expedite a temporary foster care placement with Jessica that wouldn't be processed through the system until they were sure Zane Swiegert couldn't track them as the custodial parent. Paperwork was also being drawn up to terminate Swiegert's parental rights. But again, nothing official was going forward as long as Nate and Abby were in protective custody.

Conor Wildman and his wife, Laura, were good people. Laura had taken the initiative and gotten some new clothes in the right sizes for Nate and Abby, and had picked up a couple of age-appropriate toys and games for them. Their daughter, Marie, was just a year younger than Abby, and when the family came over for dinner, the little girls played together and seemed to become fast friends.

Shadow hadn't had another seizure since the morning of Conor's interview with Nate, and she hadn't had another flashback since Garrett and the children had moved in.

It wasn't perfect. Abby communicated in her own way, but still wasn't talking to any adults. And Nate seemed to be waiting for the other shoe to drop. He'd gotten him and his sister away from Kansas City, but he rarely dropped his guard, except with the dogs. He reminded Jessica of the way she'd been even a couple of weeks ago. Happy but afraid. Confident but worried. Wanting to be free of the violence that haunted him, yet always expecting it would one day return. Jessica and Garrett had discussed their concerns with the social worker, and she promised to have a child psychologist lined up to talk with Nate and Abby as soon as it was safe to do so.

If she was being completely honest with herself, Jessica was still waiting for the other shoe to drop, too.

This morning Jessica was on the back deck, sipping an iced tea and watching Nate play the flying disk game with Toby out in the yard while Abby finished up her schoolwork at the table across from her. The little girl had lit up when Hugo brought over one of Penny's puppies as a reward for doing her schoolwork. With the promise that she'd return the puppy to the barn after lunch, Hugo had patted Abby's head and traded a salute with Nate before he climbed into his truck and headed home for the day.

The hair at the nape of her neck prickled to attention when Shadow growled from the deck beside her. One second, he was lounging in the relatively warm sunshine. The next, his hackles were up, and he'd jumped to his feet.

"Shadow?" Setting her drink down, she checked her watch. Nothing had pinged on the camera alert, indicating they had visitors. She skimmed the backyard and peered as much as she could into the trees lining the property. The puppy whimpered with concern as Shadow looked toward where Miss Eloise had shown up with her shotgun last week and growled again.

Today, she only hoped it was a lonely old woman with a shotgun.

Then she heard Rex's booming bark. Toby alerted to the sound like a call to battle and raced off into the trees. To her horror, she watched Nate take off right after him.

"Nate, stop!" Jessica was on her feet, hurrying down the steps with Shadow loping beside her. The little boy reluctantly stopped and came trudging toward her. She combed her fingers through his sweaty hair and brushed it off his face in a tender gesture he jerked away from. But there was fear trembling in his bottom lip, despite his defiance. "I'll check it out with the dogs. Get your sister in the house. You know what to do."

He glanced up at Abby, who cradled the puppy in her arms at the top of the steps. Her blues eyes darted between Jessica and her brother. Nate nodded and raced up the stairs to grab her hand. "I know."

Jessica waited until Nate had locked the back door behind them. Then she brushed her fingers across Shadow's head and issued the command. "Shadow, seek."

The dog raced into the trees, and she jogged after him.

But when she cleared the low-hanging evergreen branches, she pulled up short at the sight that greeted her. Not Miss Eloise complaining about her dogs and a dead chicken.

Parked just on the other side of her fence was Isla Gardner and a heavy-duty pickup pimped out with red and orange flames painted across the sides and tailgate. And yeah, there was some kind of short rifle on a rack in the back window of the truck. Isla looked a little pimped out herself with her bleached blond hair pulled up in a bouncy high ponytail, her painted fingernails bedazzled with sparkly jewels, and her white tank top pulled tight enough to look uncomfortable over her unnaturally perky breasts.

But the scariest thing about Isla was the tall, muscular man beside her, wearing a denim cut over a sleeveless white T-shirt. He had a sleeve of tats up and down his left arm and wore dark glasses that completely masked his eyes. He sported a brown crewcut, a long beard that would rival any '80s rock band guitarist, and he had a black skull tattooed on the side of his neck. More alarming yet, he had both hands on the top railing of Miss Eloise's fence as if he'd been about to leap over it onto Jessica's property.

"Jessica, hi." Isla greeted her with a friendly smile and reached for the bruiser's hand. "I'm showing my boyfriend around the place."

"Hey, Isla." She noted that while Isla held tight to her new man's hand, he didn't care enough to fold his around hers, as well. While that was a pitying observation compared to the way Garrett treated *her*, Jessica's focus was on the dangerous-looking man and the neighbor who'd never been this neighborly before. "What is it with your family and my animals?"

"Grandma told me she'd had a run-in with you and your dogs and Deputy Caldwell. Are you dating him?" she boldly asked.

Thinking of where Garrett had spent the last five nights, she'd have to say yes. But something told her to get this get-together over with as quickly as possible without raising any suspicion. "How's your grandmother doing?" she countered. "Taking her meds?"

"I guess." She eyed the big Anatolian shepherd, who was eyeing her. "Are you going to call your dogs off?"

"They're on my land, so no, I don't need to."

Rex paced back and forth along the fence line, barking an occasional woof when he got too close to the visitors on the other side. Toby trotted eagerly beside him, still carrying the Frisbee Nate had thrown in his mouth. Jessica could have easily called them over and ordered them to sit. But she liked the idea of having a couple of big dogs between her and her unexpected guests. She kept Shadow beside her, curling her fingers into his fur to keep herself from panicking.

After a glance from the man beside her, Isla giggled.

"Well, I figured since we were neighbors, we could come over and visit this way."

"Not unless you want Rex to take a bite out of you. He doesn't like surprises."

Isla's smile faded and she propped her hands on her hips. "Well, that's not very neighborly. What if I came over to borrow a cup of sugar for Grandma?"

"Did you?"

Finally, the behemoth spoke. "I heard about this place. You rescue dogs and turn them into attack dogs." Despite his size, he had a raspy, oddly pitched voice.

"Service dogs," she corrected. "Medical alert dogs, companion animals, sometimes a guard dog."

He turned his head, following Toby's bouncy movements. "What's that one got in his mouth?"

"Toby, come." The black Lab trotted up to her and sat. Jessica tapped the top of his muzzle. "Drop it."

She quickly scooped up the warped plastic disk and tucked it into the back of her jeans before petting the Lab and sending him back to trail after Rex. "It's a dog toy."

"Looks like a child's toy to me," he argued.

"Not if one of my dogs decides it's his to chew up." She squinted up at him, wishing she could see his eyes so that she could give Garrett and Conor a better description. "Who are you?"

"I'm with Isla."

Not an answer. But that wasn't any more suspicious than the tattoos and lack of eye contact.

"Kevie, don't be mean. I said I'd show you around Grandma's place and introduce you to the strange neighbor lady. Told you she prefers dogs to people."

She'd trade the *strange* insult for a little more information on the new boyfriend.

"How long have you two known each other?" Jessica asked, trying to keep her tone politely serious. With the matching tat, this guy had to be working with Kai Olivera. But did Isla know what was going on? Was she aiding and abetting a criminal or being taken advantage of?

"I met Kevie about a week ago at a bar up in Lone Jack." She walked her fingers up over his bulky shoulder. "I don't think I've hit it off with a guy as fast as I did with you."

The moment she touched her long nail to his lips, he grabbed her wrist and twisted it roughly down to her side. "I told you not to do that." When Isla rubbed her wrist as if his grip had hurt her, he tapped the end of her nose and flashed a quick smile. "Baby."

Isla smiled as though the endearment made everything better. "What can I say? He gets me."

Or he's using you. To get to me and the children.

Speaking of children… Suddenly, Kevie wanted to talk. "Hey, I've got a friend in the city. His kids have gone missing. Have you seen a little blonde girl about yea high?" He spread his thick fingers down by his thigh. Then raised it a few inches. "Or a boy about this big?"

With her worst fears confirmed—that this guy was looking for Nate and Abby for his pal, Olivera—she carefully schooled her voice into a friendly, yet casual tone. "We're kind of in the middle of nowhere here. Children don't just wander by. Unless they're farmers' kids. And I know most of the locals. They stop by the house to sell things for school fundraisers, that sort of thing. I've got one young man who works for me a couple times a week. But he'd be taller than what you're looking for."

"Show them the picture, Kev—baby," Isla suggested, finally grasping that he didn't want her blabbing his name to Jessica.

"Yeah." Kevie pulled a folded piece of paper from the back pocket of his jeans. He shook it open and handed it over the fence. It was a photocopy of a flyer with Nate's and Abby's school pictures Zane Swiegert must have made and distributed around the city. "That's them. You seen them around here?"

Jessica shook her head and handed it back. But the moment Kevie's hand came over the fence, Shadow growled and Rex gave him a warning bark.

The big man snatched his hand back, his cheeks growing ruddy with anger. "I'm not afraid of your dogs," he insisted.

"You don't have to be afraid of anything, unless you're up to something you shouldn't be."

He turned his face to the side and spit. Jessica was quite certain that was his opinion of a strong woman who challenged his authority. "You got a mouth on you, don't you?"

Again, she ignored the insult in favor of gaining more information. "They're beautiful children. How did they get lost?"

"They're not lost. The little cowards ran away." He pointed a stubby finger at her, and when Toby propped his front paws up on the fence, thinking he was about to make a new friend, the man shoved him away. "You see those kids, give me a call at the number on the back of that paper."

"Or call me," Isla offered, backing away as Kevie stalked back to his truck and climbed inside. "I can get a hold of him."

Isla barely had the door open and her foot on the running board before he stomped on the accelerator and sped away. She fell into the passenger seat and closed the door as gravel, grass, and other debris flew out behind the fishtailing truck.

Jessica quickly shielded her eyes and spun away. She felt the sting of debris hitting the back of her legs, and heard a yelp of pain. She was grateful for a good pair of jeans and thick boots to protect herself, but knew instantly one of the dogs had been hurt. She should feel guilty for checking Shadow first, but when he seemed fine enough to bark at the truck speeding away, she turned to the other two. With the threat gone, Rex was loping away. But Toby was limping.

"Toby! Here!" Grateful that he was still mobile, she gave him a quick once-over, then scratched him around the ears and urged him to follow her to the house. "Come on, boys. It's for your own safety as well as mine."

Jessica pulled her phone from her pocket and chased after the dogs who were already racing back to the house. She tapped the familiar number and put the phone to her ear, pushing past the trees and hurrying up to the deck.

Garrett answered after the first ring. "Jessie?"

"I need you."

From the sound of his breathing she could tell he was moving. "What's wrong?"

"A man was here. Kevie Something. Said he was Isla Gardner's new boyfriend, but I think he was just using her to get access to the property. He had a tattoo on his neck like the picture you showed me of Kai Olivera."

"Did he hurt you?"

"No, but…"

"But what?"

She stomped up the stairs to the deck, trying to catch her breath so she could talk. "He acted like he knew I was lying about the children. He spooked me. He drove away way too fast. Kicked up gravel. He nicked Toby."

Garrett swore. "I'm leaving the office right now. Get to the kids, then call Hernandez. She's on duty at the gate."

"Are you coming?" She pulled out her keys and unlocked the door.

"I'm on my way. Get inside the house. Lock the doors. Take Shadow and Toby with you. You can doctor him up inside."

"I got the guy's license plate."

"Give it to me." She rattled off the letters and numbers. "All right. I'll run this. See if we can get an ID. I'm guessing he's a known associate of Olivera's. Are the kids okay?"

"I'm not inside yet." Setting aside her fears and focusing on the lock, she got it open and shooed the dogs in ahead of her. "Nate? Abby?" She didn't immediately see them. "You don't think one of his friends got in while he was distracting me?"

"Not with Hernandez there." She hoped. She locked the door behind her and ran up the stairs to their bedroom. She worked outdoors and wasn't afraid of physical labor. But her lungs were about to burst with all this running. "Get eyes on the kids. I'm almost there. Call me right back if something's wrong."

The siren blared in the background before he ended the call. Jessica tucked her phone in her jeans and searched the bedroom. Closet. Under the bed. Behind the door. Shadow followed right on her heels, searching for the children. She dashed across the hall and shoved open the bathroom door. They'd strategized about places in the house where they could hide. This room had a door with a lock and an older tub made of porcelain-coated steel. But there was no Nate. No Abby. Her heart pounded inside her chest. She looked in the tub, in the cabinet under the sink.

"Where are you?" she muttered, looking under other beds and inside other closets. Oh, God. Had someone gotten into the house and taken the children?

She could feel the snaky tendrils of a panic attack sneaking into her head. "Shadow?"

He was at her side in an instant, leaning against her leg. She listened to him panting. She focused on his warmth. She curled her fingers into his coarse long fur and believed that she was safe. "Nate? Abby?"

She realized she was also armed with a powerful weapon. A dog's nose. "Of course." Jessica raced back into the bedroom where they'd been sleeping and scooped up Nate's pillow and pallet, holding them to Shadow's nose. She hadn't specifically trained him to do search and rescue, but she hoped he'd catch on. "Shadow, seek. Find Nate."

Understanding her meaning if not her words, Shadow trotted back down the stairs and went through the living room and ended up in the kitchen. They moved past Toby, who was curled up on Shadow's bed, licking what was no doubt a cut on his leg.

When Shadow sat down in front of the pantry door, Jessica cursed. She'd run right past it looking for the children. But when she heard a puppy whimpering from the other side of the door, she knew she'd found them. "Good boy, Shadow."

She pulled open the door. "Oh, thank God." Abby was crying, holding the puppy in her arms as she hid behind her brother. Almost dizzy with relief, Jessica reached for them. "You're safe. The man is gone."

But Nate had armed himself with the fireplace poker. "We're not going back! You can't make us!"

Jessica retreated a step and Shadow tilted his head, questioning why his new friend was threatening her. "It's okay, Shadow. Good boy." While she petted the shepherd mix, she spoke softly to the kids. "It's okay, Nate. I got rid of him. Do you know another man with a tattoo on his neck like the bald man has?"

He lowered the poker a fraction. But his eyes were wide with fear. "Did he have a long, dirty brown beard?" She nodded. "He works with the bald man. He was at the apartment when they hurt Dad." He lifted the poker and thrust it at her like a broadsword. "He can't have her, either."

For once, she ignored Shadow growling beside her. "No one is giving either of you up. The lady from Family Services said you're with me for the whole month, remember? Longer than that, if I have anything to say about it."

"If you're lying, we'll run away again. You have to at least keep Abby here."

Jessica's overtaxed heart nearly broke. "I'm not lying. I want *both* of you to stay with me."

Abby sniffed back her tears and tugged at the sleeve of her brother's shirt. "Natey, Charlie and I want out of here."

But Nate blocked her with his arm, always the protector.

Jessica reassured Shadow that she wasn't afraid and knelt in front of Nate. "Will you let Abby out? You know I won't hurt her."

All three of them startled at the sound of pounding at the door. "Jessie! It's Garrett. Let me in."

Nate relented his protective stance. He lowered the weapon as if having the other man around meant he could drop his guard a bit. "Deputy Caldwell is here?"

"I called him. He came right away when I told him about the man. He's here to help."

Abby seemed relieved to hear Garrett's voice, too. "Natey…" She slipped around her brother and ran into Jessie's arms.

"Jessie!"

She picked up the crying girl, puppy and all, and hurried to the door. "I'm coming!"

The moment she unlatched the door, Garrett pushed it open and locked it behind him. He cupped Abby's cheek and stroked Jessica's hair. "Is everyone all right?" He quickly surveyed the main floor. "Where's Nate?"

The boy came out of the pantry, still holding the poker. Garrett moved past Jessica. "Did you protect your sister the way I told you?"

Nate's eyes were glued on Garrett's. "Yes, sir. I hid us in the kitchen closet until Jessie found us."

"Good man."

"You can't give us back to our dad. The bald man will hurt her."

"That's not the plan, son." He held out his hand for the poker, and Nate reluctantly handed it over. Jessica wished Nate would let someone comfort him and allow him to be a child again, but unlike his sister, he was a touch-me-not. He seemed to appreciate and respond to Garrett's businesslike directives, though. "Jessie told me Toby got hurt. Will you help her take care of him?"

That made the boy react. "Toby got hurt?" He raced across the kitchen to kneel in front of the black Lab. "Tobes?" He probed the spot where the dog had been licking and found blood in his fur. "He's bleeding."

"Will you help Jessie doctor him up?"

The boy nodded.

Jessica carried Abby into the kitchen, drawn to Garrett's calm, strong presence, just like the children were. He petted the scruff of Charlie's neck, then held out his hands to Abby. "Will you let me hold you while

Jessie helps Nate with Toby?" Instead of answering, the little girl stretched out one arm to him, keeping the other secured around her pup. Garrett easily took them both into his arms, nestling her on the hip opposite his firearm. Then he spoke to Jessica. "Go. See if you can calm him down. I've got her. I'll need some details when you're done. I've already called the incursion in to Conor. He's sending backup, and I've got Hernandez walking the property line between here and the Gardner farm. I'll have her do a wellness check on Miss Eloise, as well."

Jessica nodded but paused to pull off Garrett's official ballcap and smooth down his hair. If the cap was off, he was staying. "Thank you for coming so quickly."

He dropped a quick kiss to her forehead. "Nobody's hurting these kids. Or you. Go." He turned away with Abby, carrying her into the living room. "Did I ever tell you the story about the puppy I had when I was little?"

"When were you little?" Abby's shy question were her first words to an adult, and Jessica fought to stem the tears that suddenly blurred her vision.

"A long time ago, sweetie. His name was Ace…"

Chapter Ten

Conor Wildman's suit collar was turned up and his jacket was drenched when Garrett opened the front door to let him into the house two nights later.

The spring rains had finally come. And while the budding trees would leaf out and the grass would turn green once it soaked up enough sun, and the farmers cheered that their crops would start growing, all Garrett could think of was that the dark, overcast sky and wall of rain gave Swiegert, Olivera, and his crew more places to hide.

The security cameras had alerted him to the detective's arrival, but it was too dark to make out who the driver was. If Officer Fox hadn't texted him to tell him Conor was pulling up to the house, Garrett would have met him at the door with his gun in his hand.

He still wore his Glock tucked into the back of his jeans. One of Olivera's men had gotten close enough to touch one of Jessie's dogs. And although Toby's injury had turned out to be no more severe than his own healing knuckles, the danger had come too close to Jessie for his comfort. So, he was armed. He was pissed.

And he was deadly. The enemy wasn't getting past him on his watch.

Conor was an ally, not an enemy, though. He folded down his collar and shook the raindrops off his suit coat before stepping inside. He toed off his wet shoes on the mat beside the door and was facing Garrett by the time he'd checked as far as he could see beyond the edge of the front porch and locked the door again.

Conor's collar was unbuttoned, and his tie was missing. The man had had a long day. "We found Zane Swiegert dead. Massive overdose. Don't know if it was accidental, suicide, or murder yet. His body's at the ME's office now."

Garrett appreciated that the detective wasn't a man who minced words. But he wasn't sure how to process the news. His gut reaction was a silent cheer that there was one less lowlife he had to worry about out there in the world. But just as quickly came the thought that somebody was going to have to tell those children, who'd already lost so much, that their father was gone. Zane Swiegert might not win any father-of-the-year awards, but he was someone whom Nate and Abby had loved. And, if Nate's account was correct, he'd done what little he'd been able to in order to help them escape his deal with Kai Olivera. It also occurred to him that their yet-to-be official foster home here with Jessie could continue for real once Olivera was behind bars and the threat to them was over.

He ended up muttering a curse and scrubbing his fingers through his hair. "Those poor kids."

He tilted his head up to where they were sleeping

and saw Jessie coming down the stairs. After baths and toothbrushing, she'd been reading them to sleep each night. He sat in on one session and had gotten caught up in the story himself. But mostly, his heart had been aching for that to be his real life—a quiet bedroom, two beautiful children snuggling up on either side of the woman he loved, tucking them in and kissing them good-night—Nate only after he'd fallen asleep and couldn't protest the mushy sign of affection. Then walking across the hall and falling into bed with said woman. They'd make out a little. Or talk. Sometimes, they'd make love. But always, the night ended with Jessie clinging to him like a second skin and him falling asleep, needing her touch like he needed his next breath.

But that wasn't his life. He was a man with a gun and a badge. Danger surrounded them; Olivera wanted to steal away Abby and kill the boy who would testify against him. And though they clearly had some type of relationship, he'd yet to hear Jessie say the three words he most needed to hear. Not *I love you.* Although, she'd already hinted at her feelings for him.

Let's do this.

Or something to the effect that she was done being cautious and ready to go all in on a relationship with him. To give him not just her body, but her heart. To trust him not just during this crisis, but for the rest of their lives.

He didn't need her to give him children. He couldn't promise that he'd never get hurt on the job. He couldn't promise that someone else who felt wronged wouldn't come after him or the people he loved again.

But he could promise to love her with everything he had until the end of his days.

He could have this life.

Tonight, she wore sweats and a hoodie, socks, and wool slippers that had lambs embroidered on them, in deference to the dampness and cooler temperature. Her hair was pulled back in a neat braid, her face was scrubbed clean, and she looked the picture of tomboyish domestic bliss he longed for.

She smiled up at Conor and shook his hand in greeting. "You look like a man who could use a hot drink. I brewed some fresh decaf."

"Actually, I'm a man who could use a beer. If you have one."

"The news is that bad, huh?" She turned into the kitchen and gestured to the table. "Have a seat and make yourself comfortable. I'll get your beer."

She popped open a bottle and set it on the place mat in front of Conor while Garrett poured them both a cup of coffee. He added cream and sugar to hers and carried them to the table, where he pulled out a chair and sat beside her.

He let her take a few sips of the hot drink to warm her up before he reached over to squeeze her hand. "Honey, Zane Swiegert OD'd. He's in the morgue."

Her fingers grew cold within his. "What about Nate and Abby? How are we going to tell them?"

He liked that she'd said *we*, and he loved that the kids' welfare was foremost in her thoughts right now.

"We'll talk about it tonight." He glanced over at Conor to make sure he wasn't speaking out of turn. "We can sit them down after breakfast and tell them tomorrow."

She nodded. "Nate will be angry. Abby will cry. I wish we could get that psychologist out here to talk to them sooner rather than later."

"I know," he sympathized. "But we can't draw that kind of attention to the house. Not yet."

Conor downed a long swallow of the tangy drink and nodded. "And in more bad news, there's a chance he wasn't a willing victim. Our medical examiner will have an answer sometime tomorrow morning."

Garrett didn't like the pale cast to her skin. She was clearly upset by the news. But he wasn't surprised to see the color flood back into her cheeks again or hear her get down to business. This woman was made of steel. "Olivera? Do you think he's responsible?"

Conor nodded. "If it turns out to be murder, he's at the top of my list. Swiegert reneged on their deal. A man in Olivera's position can't maintain his power if he allows the people who work for him to cheat him out of what he considers rightfully his."

"You're talking about a little girl."

"And drugs and money." The detective leaned forward in his chair. "This isn't a man with a conscience we're talking about. I'm building a great case against him. Now my team just has to find him and make the arrest."

"And keep anyone else who can testify against him alive," Jessie added.

Conor scrubbed his hand down his stubbled jaw and sat back. "Yeah. That, too."

Garrett kept her hand snugged in his and continued the difficult conversation. "There's no sign of Olivera or his sidekick, Kevie?" None of them laughed at the juvenile nickname for a man who was undoubtedly an enforcer for Olivera.

"Kevin Coltrane." The man had done his research. "He and Kai are cousins. He runs a custom auto shop. That could explain the light-up car you caught on tape out here, and why we're having trouble pinning Olivera to any one vehicle. He and his crew keep changing them. Coltrane and Olivera grew up in the same neighborhood, and they went into the same line of business."

"Dealing drugs?" Jessie asked.

"Kai's the brain, and Kevie's the muscle." Conor took another drink and flashed her a wry smile. "Did his girlfriend really call him that?"

"'Fraid so. He didn't like it."

"I bet not. Women are property to men like that. Not people. The only reason he'd tolerate a nickname he didn't like was if he had to put up with her for some reason."

Garrett could guess the reason. "Like he was using her to get to Jessie. He gets a general location of where the kids were last seen, then he picks up a local and uses her to find out what the people around here know."

Jessie frowned. "You think he figured out that the children are here? Do we need to move them?"

Conor answered for him. "I don't think so. If they

are watching the place, then any sudden change, like you and Jessie leaving, would only put them on alert."

Garrett agreed.

"I just wanted to come out and tell you about Swiegert in person. Let you two decide how to break the news to Nate and Abby."

"Thanks, Conor." Jessie stared down into her coffee, deep in thought about something.

The detective polished off his beer and stood. "I wish you were on my team for real, Caldwell. I appreciate your experience and wisdom. Your patience, too, for the most part," he teased, referring to the day Garrett had punched the barn. "I'm not worried about you running the protection detail here."

"Just keep me in the loop on anything else you find out."

"Will do."

The two men shook hands before Garrett walked Detective Wildman to the door and watched him dash out into the rain to slide inside his car. He drove off with a friendly wave and Garrett locked the door behind him.

When he turned, Jessie slid her arms around his waist and walked into his chest. He folded his arms around her and hugged her tight. "Talk to me, hon."

She rested her head against his neck where it met his shoulder. "I don't know how much more of this I can take. With John's death, it was a shock. Unexpected. It was scary and tragic, but I never suspected it was coming. This time I know Olivera is after Nate and Abby—sneaking onto my property, sending his goons to spy on us and intimidate me. I feel like death is coming, and all I can do is wait for it to arrive. Kai Olivera and his greed and vengeance are hunting us, circling closer. I know he's out there somewhere, watching, waiting to attack. But dreading that moment is wearing me down. What if I get careless or fall asleep at the wrong time? What if I don't see him until it's too late? Someone I care about is still going to be hurt or die." She shrugged and burrowed closer. "It's still going to be violent and tragic. Only I'm living with that knowledge for days on end. The stress is wearing a hole in my stomach. What if I fail those children?"

"Not going to happen."

"How do you know that?"

"Because I know you." He leaned back against her arms to frame her face between his hands. "You are strong and resourceful, and more devoted to the things you care about than anyone I've ever met." Her concerns reminded him a little bit of his time as a sniper. The waiting and watching for his target to appear was always the hardest part of an assignment. "You never knew Lee Palmer was coming to shoot your husband and you. But you know Kai Olivera is coming. Don't let that knowledge get stuck in your head and paralyze you. Use it to your advantage. Prepare. Have a plan of attack. You know the layout of this place better than anyone. You know what weapons you can improvise. And you have me."

She reached up to wind her fingers around his wrists. "I don't want you to get hurt, either. I think about that every day, too."

"I'm doing everything I can to be prepared, too,"

he assured her. "I'm training the kids to do the same. This time you won't be caught off guard. Try to see the hope in that. This time you'll be able to fight back."

She shook her head. "What if I'm not strong enough?"

"You, fierce Mama Dog, are stronger than you know. This is your fortress to command. You have a twelve-dog alarm system. Security cameras. Me. Heaven help Olivera if he puts his hands on you or those children."

"Miss Eloise?"

Jessica didn't like the concern she heard in Garrett's voice that evening as he answered a frantic phone call from her elderly neighbor.

She looked up from where she was setting up a dredging station to make fried chicken for dinner to meet Garrett's worried gaze. "Have you called an ambulance yet?" He interrupted whatever argument the old woman was giving. "Then you need to hang up and call 9-1-1. I think it'd be for the best. It's better to get her checked out now than to have to drive her to the emergency room later." He got up from the table where he was helping Nate with some math work and strode out of the kitchen. "No, ma'am. I'm working another job. I'm not here for your beck and call. I'll send one of my officers to your place."

"Nate. Go ahead and put away your schoolwork. Get your sister and clean up. She can help you set the table." Jessica washed her hands and grabbed a dish towel to follow Garrett into the living room.

"Is everything okay?" Nate asked solemnly, following her. He'd taken the news of his father's death better than she'd expected. There had been a few tears, but no angry outburst. But he'd been unusually subdued throughout the rest of the day. Abby, on the other hand, had been nearly inconsolable in her grief. Pretty much the only family she'd ever known, other than Nate, was gone. It had taken a visit with Penny's puppies and an exhausted nap in her arms for the little girl to be able to function again.

Jessica wouldn't lie to the boy, but she could ease any concerns he had. "It sounds like Garrett has a call about work. He may have to go take care of someone else who needs him for a while. But he'll be back. In the meantime, Officer Fox is here with us."

"Down by the end of the driveway," Nate pointed out. "It could take forever for him to get here if we need help."

"It's not that far. You'll be okay, bud." Garrett ended the call and ruffled his fingers through Nate's hair. "Go do what Jessie asked you to. I need to talk to her for a minute."

"You'll come back, right?" Nate seemed reluctant to let Garrett go.

Garrett reached out to grip Nate's shoulder. "I'm not leaving you unprotected. Jessie can handle things here for a few minutes, and I'll be right next door. Do you remember us talking about the grandma lady who lives there?" The boy nodded. "She had…an accident at her house, and I need to go over there and make sure she's okay. I'll come back just as soon as I know she's got the help she needs. I need you to stay inside the house and do whatever Jessie tells you to do."

"Wash your hands and set the table with your sister," she reminded him.

Nate turned his sad blue eyes up to her. "You won't leave us?"

Her heart twisting at the anxious request, Jessica borrowed the surprisingly apt and lovely compliment Garrett had paid her last night. "I'm the Mama Dog around this place, aren't I? Of course, I'm staying."

It was reassurance enough for Nate. He nodded, then charged up the stairs. "Ab-by!"

"Inside voice," Garrett called after him. He stuck his finger in his ear and smirked at Jessica. "I swear that boy has no volume control."

Right. Loud, rambunctious boy. Small problem in the grand scheme of things.

"Miss Eloise had an accident?" She followed Garrett to the hall tree, where he grabbed his hat. "Is she all right?"

The night sky lit up through the windows. A loud boom of thunder rattled the panes soon after. Shadow woofed from his bed by the back door. Dr. Cooper-Burke had warned that he might be more sensitive to storms since developing his idiopathic epilepsy. Jessica felt the hair on her arms stand on end in response to the electricity in the air.

"Easy." She felt Garrett's hand on her shoulder and automatically took a calming breath. She watched his chest expand and contract beneath the protective vest he wore and took two more breaths along with him. "You afraid of storms?"

"No." She reached up to clasp his wrist, to feel his

warmth and strength and know that she was okay. "Things just seem a little tense around here tonight."

"Do I need to reassure you that I'm coming back, too?"

She shook her head. "I'm not nine years old. I know duty calls. What happened to Miss Eloise?"

His face turned grim. "Actually, she was calling about Isla. Apparently, the new boyfriend assaulted her and stole the money she had in her purse."

"*Kevie* hit her? What a surprise." Jessica felt sorry for the young woman who seemed so desperate to have a man in her life that she'd settle for one who abused her. "Probably his way of breaking up with her now that he doesn't need her help to spy on the neighbors."

"I'm going to call in an officer to take over the call, but I want to head over there to make sure the premises are clear and that Kevin Coltrane isn't in the area again."

Thunder rattled the windows again as the rain poured down. "Are you sure you want to go out in this? Do you have a jacket you can put on?"

He chuckled. "Out in my truck."

"That won't do you much good. You'll get soaked."

"Hey, you survived a trip outside to batten down the kennels and close up the barn to make sure the dogs were all okay."

"That was in daylight. It's dark as pitch out there." She shivered as another bolt of lightning streaked across the sky. "Except when it does that."

He brushed his fingers over the edge of her hair and

cupped the side of her jaw and neck. "I'll be fine. You'll be fine." He leaned in to claim her mouth in a quick kiss. "Besides, if I get soaked to the skin, you'll have to strip off all my clothes and dry me off with a towel."

"You're incorrigible, old man." She mimicked his hold on her face and cupped the side of his jaw to exchange another kiss. "Go. Let me know how Isla's doing, and don't let Miss Eloise set the two of you up."

He plunked his cap on top of his head and adjusted it into place. "Not gonna happen. I'm already taken."

She caught the door when he opened it, and even with the depth of the porch, she felt the cold rain splashing against her face. "What if this is some kind of ploy to get you away from the house so we're vulnerable here?"

Garrett turned at the edge of the porch and came back to her, grasping her face between his hands and tilting her gaze up to his. "You got this, Mama Dog. You've shown me that you can handle anything." He leaned in to kiss her again, quickly, but much more thoroughly. Then he was backing away. "Plus, I'll be back. Believe that. I will always come back to you."

She caught a brief flash of light as he opened the door to his truck. Then his headlights came on and he turned in her driveway to disappear into the night.

"He's coming back," she whispered. Then she felt Shadow's warm body pressed against her side. He must have sensed her anxiety all the way out here. "Right, boy?" She stroked her fingers through his dampening hair. "He's coming back really soon?"

Maybe it was the storm. Maybe his sharp ears had

heard something that she could not. Maybe it was only something a dog could sense. But for the first time since she'd begun to train him, Shadow whimpered beside her.

Chapter Eleven

Jessica knew the exact moment her world changed again.

Her phone pinged in her pocket.

She pulled it out and waited for a few seconds for Officer Fox or Garrett himself to call and let her know that someone she knew had turned into her driveway.

She waited.

And waited.

Her pulse rate kicked up a notch.

No one was calling.

"Shadow?" She called the dog to her side, and he answered immediately. She scratched her fingers around his ears, thinking, thinking.

Oh, hell. Her instincts screamed at her that something was wrong. If she was a dog, she would have barked.

She whirled around to the children who were debating about where to put the silverware around the plates on the table.

"Nate! Abby!" Abby startled and dropped a fork on the floor as she grabbed them both by the hand and pulled them into the living room. "Get upstairs. Run. Lock yourself in the bathroom and get down inside the tub. Don't peek out. Don't go anywhere else."

Okay. Not helping. Calm down.

She inhaled a deep breath and bent so she was closer to their heights, even as she tugged them along to the stairs. "Nate, you are in charge of your sister. Make sure she stays quiet. Make sure she stays hidden." Before Abby's protesting whine fully formed, she gave the little girl an order, too. "You are in charge of your brother. Make sure he does everything I say."

Nate stopped and squeezed her hand. "The bald man's here, isn't he."

"Yes, Nate. I think so. We don't have much time."

"Where's Deputy Caldwell?" he asked, latching on to Abby with his other hand.

"He's coming. He's on his way."

"Can Shadow—?"

"No." She answered a little too harshly. "I need him with me."

"He'll keep you safe, Jessie," the little boy whispered.

Jessica pressed a kiss to both their foreheads whether they liked it or not and pushed them toward the stairs. "Lock yourself in the bathroom. Now."

Abby tugged on her brother's hand. "She said we have to go, Natey. It's my job to make you go. Come on."

Good girl. "Stay completely quiet so no one knows you're there. Don't come out for anyone except Garrett or me. Nate, wait." She pushed her phone into the boy's hand. "Text Garrett and tell him we need him. No talking. Just text."

"I thought you said he was coming."

"He is." She hoped. "Tell him to hurry."

She glanced through the windows beside the front

door and saw a weird, rectangular light floating up her driveway. What was that? It was hard to make sense of what she was seeing through all the rain.

"Come with us." Nate tugged on her arm, begging her to hide, too.

"No, sweetie." She pulled him to her in a brief hug. "Mama Dog has to take care of business. Lock the door. Hide. Text Garrett. Go!"

The children ran up the stairs. She waited for the sound of the bathroom door closing. Locking.

She ran past the front windows and her stomach dropped down to her toes. "Oh, no. God no."

The weird lights made sense now. They were the underglow lights of the souped-up car she'd captured on her video camera that first night they'd rushed Shadow to the vet and Garrett had stayed with her. She'd bet anything that the two bulky figures she'd seen on camera were Kai Olivera and his big bruiser buddy, Kevin Coltrane.

They were here.

They were here to take Abby and kill Nate. Probably Jessica, too.

Sparing a thought for Officer Fox, she wondered if he'd been called away or if the skull cousins had disabled him somehow. Or something worse.

No time. No time.

Garrett had reminded her that she had time to prep for their arrival, time to formulate a plan of attack. She'd lost a family once before to unspeakable violence.

But she wouldn't lose this odd little family of survivors.

She ran back to the kitchen, searched for those improvised weapons Garrett had mentioned. There were
two prime candidates sitting right there on top of the
stove. She cranked the heat beneath the cast iron skillet
where she was heating up the oil for the fried chicken.

Then she picked up the chopping knife and went
back to work cutting the chicken into even smaller
pieces.

GARRETT PLACED THE bag of frozen peas over the bruise
swelling on Isla Gardner's cheek and called for an ambulance himself.

With both women talking at once, it was hard to
make sense of all the details about what had happened.
But he could get the gist of their story.

Isla had indeed been smacked around a bit. Besides
the mark on her face, she had bruises that fit the span
of a large man's hand around her wrist. Even though
she tried to defend Kevin Coltrane, Eloise informed
him that Olivera's hulking sidekick had been to the
house and robbed her, as well. Most interestingly, he'd
threatened to hit the octogenarian if she didn't allow
him to park his stupid truck at her place.

And Isla said her boyfriend had been insistent that
her grandmother call Garrett for help, that it would
make *Kevie* happy if the old guy next door answered
their call for help. The old guy wouldn't be as big a
threat as a younger officer, so she'd agreed. And she
really wanted to make *Kevie* happy so he'd come back
to her. It was just a ploy to get Garrett away from the
house, a plan to leave Jessie and the children unpro-

tected. He seriously doubted Coltrane ever planned to see Isla again, and she should be thanking her lucky stars that he was getting out of her life.

Once Maya Hernandez had arrived to take the official report from the Gardner women, and the EMTs were checking Eloise's blood pressure and Isla's injuries, Garrett drove his truck along the bumpy gravel of Eloise's driveway and turned to follow the rail fence that bordered Jessie's property.

His suspicions paid off when he found the white truck decorated with flames she had described parked to make a quick getaway with its tailgate facing the fence. A quick check of the plate number on his truck's laptop confirmed that it was Kevin Coltrane's truck. He hadn't been interested in Isla Gardner at all, maybe not even in the money he'd stolen from the two women. This was about finding the children and gaining access to the house while bypassing the security camera and guard at the front gate. It might also have something to do with approaching the house from the side where no dogs would detect an intruder. Even Big Rex wouldn't be able to stop them, because he was locked up in the barn due to the storm.

A bolt of lightning lit up the area well enough for Garrett to confirm that the truck was empty.

So, where were Coltrane and Olivera?

Pulling his cap low over his forehead and snapping his jacket all the way up to the neck, Garrett opened his truck door and stepped out into the deluge. He was soaked to the skin almost immediately and gave a brief thought to the teasing remark he'd given Jessie about drying him off. But he was more focused on finding the answer to the mystery of Coltrane's truck. A broken window on a summer cabin, a broken latch on a chicken coop or storage room—those could be attributed to two runaways looking for food to eat and a warm place to sleep at night.

But a truck parked in the back acres of a woman's land she didn't even farm anymore hinted at something much more sinister.

He discovered it when he reached the back of the pickup truck. The newly replaced railing had been torn down again, and the chain links had been cut through on Jessie's side of the fence. The hair on the back of Garrett's neck pricked to attention like it had that day in Afghanistan when he'd spotted the kid with the bomb. Things were about to go really bad very, very quickly.

He pulled out his phone and called Levi Fox.

No answer.

He jogged back to his truck and called the young officer again.

No answer.

"Damn it, Fox, where are you?"

Garrett's next call was to Dispatch, warning them of a possible officer down and requesting backup at K-9 Ranch. He told them to notify Conor Wildman at KCPD, as well.

He debated for about two seconds whether to take the long drive back to the highway, then go next door and turn in the long drive up to Jessie's house—or he could take the same shortcut across her land the way he suspected Coltrane had.

He grabbed his rifle off the rack in the back of his truck cab, leaped the fence, and ran.

"DROP THE KNIFE."

With the fury of the storm subsiding to a steady fall of rain, Jessica had no problem hearing that the house was quiet. The children had done exactly as she asked and weren't making a sound.

Stay hidden. Stay safe.

She'd also heard the shatter of breaking glass at her back door, even the lock turning as the intruder reached inside to unlock the door. Shadow barked and raced to the door, but she called him back to her side. Thankfully, he obeyed.

She was down to diced chicken bites now, and still she kept cutting.

Jessica glanced over to see a gun pointed at her. Shadow growled and snapped at the armed man, desperately fighting his basic instinct to go after the intruder. But she was too good, Shadow was too smart, and Kevin Coltrane would never know what hit him by the time they were done with him.

"I said, put down the knife, lady."

She eyed the oil shimmering, rippling in the heavy skillet. "Hello, *Kevie.*"

"I don't like to be called that."

Shadow snarled and she knew he was moving closer. "Why not? Are you going to manhandle me the way you did Isla? What do you want with me?"

"The knife."

The gun barrel pressed against the side of her neck was wet with rain and felt ice cold.

Her breath hitched in her chest. Shadow's ears lay down flat on his head.

She felt her pulse beat against the cold steel of that gun.

"I ain't playin', lady."

"Okay. Okay." Not wanting to test the limits of the Olivera enforcer too hard, she dutifully set the knife down on top of the counter, right next to a pair of oven mitts. "There. I'm not armed anymore. Who brings a knife to a gunfight, anyway, right?"

Her laugh sounded as forced as it felt.

"Shut up, already."

He smacked the butt of the gun against her temple and she tumbled on top of the raw chicken on the counter, her skull throbbing and her vision spinning. The blow must have split her skin because blood was dripping into her right eye.

"You idiot. I need her conscious. I'll make her tell me where they are if they're not here."

"She wouldn't drop the knife," the big man protested. "You want her to stab me with it?"

"Find those kids. Now!"

How had she missed the second man walking in behind Kevie? Jessica pushed herself upright, feeling nauseous as a pair of skull tattoos swam through her vision. Olivera himself. Kai Olivera.

But the other man, Kevin Coltrane, was walking away, doing the boss's bidding.

No, no, no! He was leaving the kitchen. Moving closer to Nate and Abby.

The time was now or never.

"Shadow, now!" The dog lunged at the second man's outstretched hand, clamping down with enough force to break the skin and force the gun he held from his hand.

"Damn mutt! Kevin!"

A gunshot rang out and Shadow yelped. "Shadow!" She foolishly charged after Olivera as he shook himself free of the dog's bite and kicked him toward the door. The second yelp tore through her heart. "Don't you hurt my dog!"

"I got the door." *Kevie* had circled around the island. Good. Forget the kids upstairs.

The two men wrestled the snarling, whining dog out into the rain and slammed the door shut behind him. While she mourned whatever had been done to Shadow, she sent up a prayer of thanks that he'd been able to defend her.

Two weapons gone. Two to go.

She hoped Nate had gotten hold of Garrett. She'd defend those children to her last breath, but she wouldn't last long against two armed men.

With her aim severely hampered by her spinning equilibrium, she picked up the hot mitts and grabbed the skillet.

"What is wrong with you, lady? Siccing your dog on Kai?" The big man grabbed a towel off the counter and tossed it to Olivera to stanch the wounds on his hand.

When he turned back to her, she hurled the hot oil at his face.

He screamed and wiped at the oil dripping down the front of him, burning his hands and losing his gun in the process. With his skin literally burning and peeling off his cheeks, he collapsed to his knees. Jessie swung the skillet again, this time cracking its heavy weight over the top of his head. He dropped like a stone, unconscious.

Shadow barked outside and scratched at the door. She heard the other dogs answering the alarm in the distance.

One down.

She raised her improvised weapon to strike again, but Olivera had disappeared. Then something hot and sharp and distinctly unsanitary sliced across her arm. Blood seeped up and pooled across her skin. She cried out in pain and let the pan clatter to the floor.

A heavy hand gripped her upper arm and spun her around. "I'm tired of playing these games." He shoved her against the island and bent her back partway across it. Spittle sprayed across her face as he held her own carving knife to her throat. She felt the edge of the blade prick her skin and knew she was bleeding again. "The Swiegerts are here someplace. Tell me where to find them."

"I don't know what you're talking about. You broke into my home. I'm defending myself."

Another cut. She flinched away from the burning pain. "You're not a dumb broad. Don't play dumb with me."

Fine. "I won't tell you."

"Talk, lady. Nate and Abby are mine."

Her back screamed at the angle he forced her into at the edge of the granite counter. "They don't belong to you. Their father is dead."

"Yeah. Because I pumped him so full of prime product—at my own expense—that his head damn near exploded."

Was she about to pass out? Had she heard him right? "You killed him?"

"Don't pump me for information, lady. I'm gonna cut your tongue out, and you won't be able to tell anybody anything." He pressed his forearm against her windpipe. If she didn't die of blood loss, he could strangle her to death. "Where are they?"

"I don't know."

"That's a load of crap. You got about fifteen seconds, and your boyfriend will be coming home to a dead body."

She was getting light-headed. Losing blood. Not breathing right.

She needed more time for backup to arrive. Garrett would save them. He'd promised. "They're not here."

"Where!"

Jessica saw the red laser dot spotting Kai Olivera's temple. But he did not.

"Tell me!"

Jessica turned her head and glass shattered as Olivera's brain splattered across her new kitchen cabinet.

With one last burst of strength, she shoved him off her and collapsed. She was crawling between bodies, blood and an oil slick when the door swung open again and Shadow burst in, with Garrett right behind him.

"Jessie? Jessie!"

Shadow came straight to her and licked her face. Jessica plopped back on her bottom and pulled the sopping wet dog onto her lap. "Did he shoot you, baby? Where are you hurt? You saved Mama. Good boy. Good boy."

"Jessie?" Garrett pointed the barrel of his sniper rifle at Olivera, then kicked his body away from her. "You're bleeding. How bad are you hurt?" Next, he trained the rifle on *Kevie's* prone body. When there was no reaction, he knelt beside the bearded bully and felt for a pulse. Apparently, he could still detect one because he sat back to pull out his handcuffs and locked them around the big man's wrists. Then he turned off the burner on the stove and crouched in front of her. His hand gently caressed her cheek. "Jessie, honey, you need to talk to me." He snatched a towel from the countertop and pressed it against the wound at her temple.

She winced at the pressure on the open wound, then wrapped her fingers around his wrist to stop his frantic movements. "I'm okay. Garrett, I'm okay. Probably need to see an ER. Shadow, too. But I'm okay." She found those loving green eyes narrowed with concern. Her sweet, brave, warrior man. Oh, how she loved him. She cupped his cold, wet cheek. "Get the kids. Upstairs bathroom. They were good as gold, did exactly what I asked." He hesitated. "Go. I told them not to come out for anyone but you or me. And I can't... I can't do that right now."

"Jessie, you're scaring me."

"Go. Make sure they're all right. I need to rest a minute. Shadow will stay with me. Right, boy?"

He scrubbed his hand over the dog's head. "Take good care of her, pal. I need her."

Then he was on his feet. He slipped the rifle over his shoulder and charged the stairs. "Nate! Abby!"

She heard a scramble of footsteps and shouts of "Garrett!"

When she saw them again, he carried a child in each arm and turned toward the kitchen.

"No!" she shouted, stopping him in his tracks. She glanced at the blood and death around her and knew some of it was on her. "Don't let them back here. I don't want them to see any of this."

"Jessie?" Abby called to her.

"I'm okay, baby," she answered, praying her shaky voice didn't worry the little girl. "Go with Garrett."

Lights were flashing through the windows now. Backup was here. The cavalry had arrived.

The front door closed. Jessie leaned back against the counter and closed her eyes, inhaling the pungent, normal, wonderful scent of wet dog and thanking God, the spirits of John and her baby, and any other powers that be that she was alive. Nate and Abby were alive. The threat was over.

When she opened her eyes again, Garrett was kneeling beside her. He picked her up in his arms, dog and all, and carried her out to the front porch and down the steps to the waiting ambulance. He set her on the gurney and the EMTs quickly moved to load her inside to get her out of the rain.

Abby was there, bundled in a silver reflective blanket. She climbed onto the gurney and snuggled beneath

Jessie's unblemished arm to rest her head against Jessie's breast. Nate eyed her shyly, then climbed up on the other side, his hand immediately going to Shadow's head to pet him.

The EMTs were already tearing open sterile bandages and pressing them against the cuts on her arm and neck. One shined a flashlight in her face, checking for pupil reaction, then asked her to follow his finger with her eyes. "Slight concussion. She'll need some stitches."

Garrett was the last one to climb on board the crowded ambulance several minutes later. "Conor's here. He'll handle the crime scene. We can answer questions and fill out reports later. Officer Fox had his head bashed in, but he's going to make it. He's on another ambulance. I talked to Hugo. He and Soren will come over and check on all the dogs. I called Hazel Cooper-Burke. She'll meet us at the hospital to take care of Shadow." He reached back to pull the doors shut. "Let's go."

"Sir, that dog can't come—"

"That dog is part of this family," Garrett snapped. "We all go."

Surrendering to his stubborn determination to keep them all together—if not to the badge of authority he wore—the EMT passed the word up that they were ready to leave.

As the ambulance headed down her long driveway, Garrett took a seat on the other side of Abby, holding the little girl between them, reaching over to tag his hand at the nape of Jessica's neck and feather his fingers into her hair at the root of her braid. When the EMTs took a break in tending to her injuries, he leaned in and captured her lips in a sweet, lingering kiss. She cupped the side of his jaw and held on, absorbing every bit of love he had to give her. Garrett Caldwell was warmth. He was strength. He was her future.

"I thought I was going to lose you." He carefully found a spot to rest his forehead against hers.

"You're not going to lose me, Garrett," she vowed. "Ever."

In the crowded ambulance, there was only the two of them. She was injured. She was exhausted. But she was surrounded by love, and she was happy. Finally. Fully. Happy.

He pulled away slightly, a shade of doubt clouding his eyes. "What are you saying?"

"It hurts to love again, to take that risk. But it doesn't hurt to love you."

Abby got squished between them and the EMTs politely looked away as Jessie leaned over to kiss the man she loved.

A small throat cleared behind her, and she looked down into Nate's sweet blue eyes. They were smiling—almost. "Are you two going to be kissing every time we leave the room?"

Garrett chuckled. "Possibly. I might kiss Jessie in front of you, too. Are you okay with that?"

Nate gave the proposition some considerable thought. "Yeah. But not all the time, okay? It's kind of gross."

Garrett extended his arm and shook the boy's hand. "I can work with that."

Garrett shifted so that his arm slipped around her

back and his hand rested on Nate's shoulder. He dropped a kiss to the top of Abby's head, tying them all together as a family.

The attack had come.

And she'd survived.

Again.

Only this time, with this man, there would be a happily-ever-after.

* * * * *

Look for more books in USA TODAY
bestselling author Julie Miller's
Protectors at K-9 Ranch miniseries
coming soon!